Feral

Monica Lynne Chase

Introduction: The Legend of the 13th Child

In the depths of the Pine Barrens, where shadows stretch long and even the bravest animals go silent at dusk, there lies a story that few dare to tell, and fewer still survive to hear. It's a tale older than memory, whispered around fires and muttered in low voices, a warning to those who stray too far into the woods. They say the forest has a life of its own, that it breathes and watches, that its branches sway not with the wind but with something darker, something that waits.

In these woods, the trees remember. They remember a time when people were afraid, when those who dared to live near the Pine Barrens knew better than to wander alone at night. For hidden deep within, beneath the twisted roots and the black soil, a shadow stirs—a thing born from the old curses and unkept promises. This is the story of the 13th child, the one born under a dark prophecy, destined to be both sacrifice and hunter.

The elders of the nearby village still remember the warnings passed down from ancestors who dared to settle near the PineBarrens. They speak of a child not quite human, a spirit of both flesh and shadow, fated to be the forest's servant, claimed by the woods before her first breath. They say she is bound to the land itself, that her bloodline is marked by an ancient pact, a curse that spans generations. Some call her the devil's daughter; others say she is the forest's chosen. But all agree—she is nothing like the others.

For thirteen children came into this world, but twelve never lived to leave it. And on the blood of those who died before her, the 13th child was born—wild, untamed, a creature of soil and bone who belonged to the Pine Barrens as much as the oldest oak. She walks between worlds, eyes dark as the midnight trees, a part of the forest's shadow. She is drawn deeper into the woods with each passing year, called to its heart by whispers only she can hear.

The people of the village avoid the forest, especially when the winds blow cold and sharp, carrying voices that sound almost human. They tell their children not to wander off the path, to keep away from the trees that seem to watch and listen. But the Pines, they have a way of claiming what they want. And when the night is at its darkest, when the moon hides behind the clouds, it is said that the 13th child roams. She is not alone, for the woods have granted her companions—shadows that slither through the trees, a darkness that clings to her like a second skin.

So, remember, if you dare to enter these woods, do not follow the murmurs or heed the songs of the trees. Do not look too closely at the branches that sway without wind or the roots that twist as if they hunger. And should you ever see her—a girl with feral eyes, barefoot and wild, who looks at you with a gaze that is both child and beast—turn back, for the Pines have found you. The 13th child has marked you, and there are some places where no one hears you scream.

Table of Contents

Chapter 1: Born of the Pines

The deep woods of the Pine Barrens didn't simply shelter her; they shaped her. As a child, she crawled through the underbrush, feeling the sharp twigs under her bare hands, her breath matching the rhythm of the wind weaving through the towering pines. Her siblings chattered to one another, their voices bouncing off the trees, but she was silent.

She didn't need words. The rustle of a squirrel in the canopy above, the soft crunch of dead leaves beneath the weight of a nearby deer—these were the sounds she understood. Her senses were always tuned to the forest's frequency, not the human ones.

While her brothers and sisters would return to the tiny wooden cabin they called home, she lingered in the woods. Long after twilight bled into the blackness of night, she would crouch beside a fox's den, watching the creature hunt with patience, imitating the predator's stillness. She felt more kinship with the fox than with her own blood.

When her siblings ran through the woods, they tripped on roots and cursed the trees. But she learned to move as they did, swift, silent, part of the forest rather than an intruder.

It wasn't long before her parents noticed the difference. Their youngest, wildest daughter, whose eyes glimmered like an animal's, wasn't interested in the world beyond the pines. She refused to sleep in the cabin and, on some nights, wouldn't return at all. They would find her curled in a hollowed log, dirt streaked across her face, her breaths deep and steady, as if she belonged more to the earth than the family who birthed her.

Her mother often watched from the cabin doorway, a frown etched deep into her weathered face. The other children were lively, playing games near the house or chasing each other through the undergrowth. But the youngest—she was different. There was a wildness in her that even the other children sensed. They learned to leave her be, and her father, gruff and practical, stopped trying to drag her back inside each night.

"She's like the animals," her mother would whisper to herself, shaking her head, uncertain whether to be proud or afraid.

And the girl was. From the moment her tiny feet could carry her through the brush, she was drawn away from the warmth of home and into the cool embrace of the woods. She would lie under the canopy of trees, her face turned toward the sky, eyes unblinking as she traced the path of clouds drifting past. When the wind rustled the branches, she listened as if the forest itself spoke to her in a language only she could understand.

By the time her siblings reached adolescence, they were talking of leaving the woods. Her older brother dreamed of working in the nearby town's sawmill, and her sister wanted to work on one of the farms just beyond the treeline. The idea of being anywhere but the Pine Barrens seemed absurd to the youngest daughter. Why would they want to leave? She belonged to the woods, and she could never imagine herself outside its reach.

The animals, too, seemed to know. It wasn't just the foxes or deer that passed through her life like fleeting shadows. Birds lingered near her more often than her siblings. She would sit with her back against a tree, her eyes wide open, watching the slow flutter of a bird's wings as it landed on a nearby branch, its head cocked in curiosity. Her movements were slow and measured, careful never to startle. And when the animals didn't flee, she felt a triumph—a wordless connection that made her heart swell.

But there were other things that made their presence known in the forest—things that weren't as easy to see.

At night, when the darkness was so complete it swallowed everything, she could feel it. A presence, lurking just beyond the trees. It moved like the wind, silent and untouchable. The others never sensed it, but she did. The hair on the back of her neck would rise, her heart would pound harder, and she would crouch low, watching, waiting. She wasn't afraid—at least not in the way others would be. It felt more like a challenge, a game. Whatever was out there watched her, but she watched it back.

Her family could never understand this pull. They only saw the surface, the dirt under her fingernails, the tangles in her hair, the wild gleam in her eyes. As her siblings grew older and more distant, the wild child remained behind, fading from their world of human chatter and plans. They whispered about her when they thought she couldn't hear.

"Maybe she's not right in the head," her sister said once, casting a nervous glance at her younger sibling crouched in the clearing.

The girl heard, but she didn't care. Let them think what they wanted. Words meant little to her anyway.

The days passed, and her connection to the forest deepened. She moved effortlessly through the underbrush, barefoot and silent, her eyes sharper than ever, her senses honed to a point. She could smell the rain before it came.

She could smell the rain before it came, feel the shift in the air before the storm clouds gathered. The forest revealed its secrets to her—secrets her family could never see. She knew where the foxes burrowed, where the deer grazed at dusk, and where the owls perched to watch the world beneath them. The woods became her sanctuary, her only companion in a world that grew increasingly distant.

Her family continued to change. Her siblings, now nearly grown, had outgrown the woods. They spoke of jobs in town, of futures that extended beyond the treeline. Her older brother, Will, spent long days talking with the men who passed through the edge of the woods, offering help for a few coins. Her sister, Clara, had taken to visiting the farms beyond the Pine Barrens, learning the ways of the town, the work, the people. Soon, the family cabin would be a temporary place for them—a fading part of their past.

But the youngest didn't care about their plans. She only listened to the sounds of the woods. The rustle of leaves, the distant call of an owl, the rhythm of the forest filling her mind with every step she took. She was a creature of this world, more comfortable in the wild than in the home that felt more and more like a cage.

Her mother's worried glances were constant now. There were whispers of sending her to the town, to learn the ways of "proper" life. But that talk faded when her father shook his head, his voice rough and final.

"She's not like the others," he said. "Let her be."

And so they did. She was left to roam the woods, to sleep beneath the trees, her body coated in dirt, her hair tangled and wild. She grew stronger, faster, more attuned to the rhythms of nature than her own humanity.

But the forest wasn't always a place of safety.

One evening, as the sun dipped low and cast the woods in a deep orange glow, she ventured farther than she ever had before. The trees became denser, the air heavier. There was a part of the woods her parents had always warned her to avoid—the far side, where the trees grew thick and old, where the shadows seemed to move on their own. But she was curious. And she had never been afraid of the dark.

The deeper she went, the more the world around her seemed to shift. The familiar calls of the forest animals faded, replaced by a heavy, oppressive silence. The air grew still, and even the wind seemed to retreat from this place.

Her heart pounded in her chest, not from fear, but from the thrill of the unknown. Her eyes scanned the shadows, her ears straining to catch the faintest sound.

And then, she felt it again—that presence. The one that had watched her from the edges of the forest, lurking just beyond her reach. It was closer now. She could feel it, pressing in on her from all sides.

She crouched low, her fingers digging into the earth, her breath slow and steady. She wasn't afraid. She was ready.

The forest around her seemed to hold its breath, the trees standing still as sentinels, watching the scene unfold. Then, out of the corner of her eye, she saw movement. A shadow, darting between the trees, too quick and fluid to be anything human. It circled her, staying just out of sight, its presence a constant, creeping thing.

But she didn't move. She remained perfectly still, her eyes sharp, her senses heightened. Whatever it was, it wanted her to run. It wanted her to be afraid. But she wasn't. She was something different. Something more.

A low growl rumbled from the shadows. A challenge.

She rose to her feet slowly, her muscles coiled like a predator's, her eyes locked on the darkness where the presence lurked.

It stepped into view, just at the edge of the clearing. The shape was indistinct, blending into the darkening woods, but its eyes—those gleaming, animalistic eyes—fixed on her. She stared back, unblinking, refusing to flinch.

For a long moment, they stood, predator and prey, facing each other. But she was no prey.

Without a sound, the shadow turned and disappeared into the trees, leaving her alone in the clearing. The forest exhaled, the wind picking up again, rustling the leaves as though the encounter had never happened.

She remained still for a long time, her heart finally slowing, her breath steady. Whatever it was, it had seen her. Acknowledged her. But it hadn't attacked. Not yet.

She turned back toward home, the path through the woods familiar beneath her feet. But as she walked, a new awareness settled over her. There was something else in the woods. Something that knew her as she knew it.

And it was waiting.

Chapter 2: The Eyes in the Dark

The presence became her constant forest companion. At first, it lingered at the edges, barely there, a shadow that melted into the background of the forest. But as the days passed, it grew bolder. She felt it watching, always watching, from the moment she woke to the time she curled up beneath the stars. It was silent but never absent. And though she could never catch more than a fleeting glimpse, she knew it was there.

It wasn't a creature of the woods, at least not like the others she had come to understand. This was different, something older. Something darker.

One night, as she lay under the cover of leaves, her head resting against the smooth bark of an oak, she awoke suddenly. There was no sound to rouse her, no snap of a twig or shuffle of paws, but the air had changed. The forest had gone unnaturally quiet, the usual chorus of insects and night birds conspicuously absent.

She sat up, her breath slow and controlled, her eyes scanning the darkness. It was there again, closer this time. She could feel its eyes on her, sharp and probing, cutting through the night. She remained still, her heart beating steadily, refusing to show fear.

Minutes passed, then hours. The presence didn't move, and neither did she. They were locked in a silent standoff, both waiting for the other to make the first move. But nothing came. Slowly, the world around her began to stir again. The crickets resumed their song, the wind rustled through the trees, and the oppressive weight of the encounter lifted.

But even as she lay back down, she knew it was far from over.

The following days were marked by the presence's increasing proximity. No longer content to lurk in the shadows, it moved closer, bolder, watching her in daylight as well as in the dark. Sometimes she would catch a glimpse of it—a flash of movement just beyond the trees, a shadow where there should be none. Other times, she would hear the faintest whisper of sound, like a breath too soft to be real.

But it was real. She was certain of that.

Her siblings, lost in their own world of dreams beyond the woods, noticed nothing. They carried on as if the forest held no secrets, oblivious to the tension that had woven itself into her days. She didn't tell them. They wouldn't understand.

But her father—he saw something.

One evening, as the light faded from the sky, her father found her at the edge of the woods. She had been sitting in silence, her gaze fixed on a spot between the trees where she knew the presence was watching. He approached quietly, as he always did, and sat beside her.

"You've been spending more time out here than usual," he said gruffly, though there was a softness in his voice that was rarely there.

She didn't respond at first, her eyes never leaving the shadows.

"There's something in the woods," she finally said, her voice low and even.

Her father didn't laugh or dismiss her as others might have. He stared into the trees, his jaw set in a hard line.

"I know," he said after a long pause. "I've felt it too."

She turned to him, surprised. Her father, the man who had always been so rooted in practicality, was acknowledging what she had only dared to whisper to herself.

"What is it?" she asked, her voice barely a whisper.

He shook his head, his face grim. "Something old. Something that's been here longer than us. You're not the first to feel it, and you won't be the last."

He stood then, placing a heavy hand on her shoulder. "Stay away from it. Whatever it is, it's not for us."

But she couldn't stay away. The pull of the presence was too strong, too deep. It wasn't just a thing to be feared; it was something that called to her, beckoning her deeper into the woods, into the unknown.

The following night, she ventured farther than she ever had before. The moon hung high, casting long shadows across the forest floor as she slipped through the trees, her movements soundless. The presence was there, as it always was, watching, waiting.

She moved toward it, no longer afraid, no longer cautious. She needed to know what it was, what it wanted. The deeper she went, the thicker the air became, heavy and humid, as if the very atmosphere were pressing down on her.

And then she saw it.

At the edge of a clearing, standing just beyond the reach of the moonlight, was a figure. Not a man, not an animal—something in between. Its body was tall and thin, almost skeletal, with long limbs that seemed to stretch unnaturally. Its eyes—those same gleaming eyes she had seen in the darkness—were fixed on her, glowing faintly in the dim light.

She froze, her breath catching in her throat. For the first time, she felt a flicker of something close to fear. But she didn't run. She stood her ground, her eyes locked on the figure.

It stepped forward, its movements slow and deliberate, as though it were testing her, gauging her reaction. But she didn't flinch. She stared back, unblinking, her heart pounding in her chest.

The figure paused, just at the edge of the light, and for a long moment, they stood in silence, the world around them holding its breath.

And then, in a voice that seemed to come from everywhere and nowhere, it spoke.

"You are not like the others."

Her heart skipped a beat, the words sinking deep into her mind. It knew her. It had been watching, waiting. And now, it had come for her.

Chapter 3: The Voice of the Pines

The voice lingered in the air, thick and heavy like the mist that sometimes rolled through the forest at dawn. It was not human. It carried a resonance, an ancient quality that made the hair on her arms stand on end. She had spent her whole life in the woods, had learned the language of the animals and the rhythm of the earth beneath her feet— but this voice, this thing, was different. It belonged to the forest in a way she never could.

The figure did not move closer, but its presence was suffocating. It stood just beyond the light, its long, bony fingers twitching at its sides. The moonlight barely touched it, and what little did only made it more shadow than substance. Its eyes—those terrible, glowing eyes—never left her.

"You are not like the others," it repeated, the voice curling around her like smoke. "You hear the whispers. You feel the pull. You are meant to stay."

Her breath hitched in her throat. Meant to stay? She had always felt it, the connection to the woods, the way she belonged here more than anywhere else. But now, hearing it spoken aloud, it sounded less like fate and more like a trap. Something inside her stirred—an instinct, a primal warning. She took a step back.

The figure tilted its head, as if amused. "Do you think you can leave?" it asked, its voice low and dangerous. "You've been mine since the day you first set foot here. The others—they flee because they do not belong. But you... you are the forest."

She shook her head, her mind racing. This wasn't real. It couldn't be. Her heart pounded, the blood rushing in her ears, drowning out the stillness of the woods around them. She had always loved this place, had always felt it was home—but now it felt like a cage, like a living thing that had been waiting to close in on her.

"I don't belong to anyone," she whispered, more to herself than to the figure. But the thing heard her, and its laugh—a soft, bone-chilling sound—echoed through the clearing.

"Oh, but you do," it said, stepping forward ever so slightly. "You belong to me. You always have and you always will."

The ground beneath her feet seemed to shift, the roots of the trees creeping closer, the branches overhead swaying ominously. The air thickened, the once familiar scent of pine now tinged with something bitter, something rotten. She glanced around, desperate for a way out, but the forest had closed in around her. The path she had followed was gone, swallowed by the undergrowth.

Panic clawed at her chest. Her mind screamed at her to run, to escape, but her body was frozen in place. The figure, sensing her fear, moved closer. Its long limbs moved unnaturally, like a marionette pulled by invisible strings.

"You can fight it," it whispered, its voice softer now, almost soothing. "But you will lose. The forest is in your blood. It has been waiting for you, shaping you. You were never meant to be like them. You were never went to leave"

She trembled, her hands clenched into fists, nails digging into her palms. Her father's warnings echoed in her mind. Stay away from it. Whatever it is, it's not for us.

But it was, it was for her. That much was clear now.

The figure stopped just at the edge of her reach, its eyes glowing brighter, its presence overwhelming. The shadows around it seemed to twist and writhe, as though the darkness itself was alive. The voice was in her head now, filling her thoughts, drowning out everything else.

"You've seen the truth," it said. "You've felt it. The wild in you, the animal—that is your nature. The others? They are nothing. They will leave. They will die. But you—you can become something more. Something greater."

Her breath came in shallow gasps, her chest tightening. The figure reached out a hand, its long, claw-like fingers beckoning her forward.

"All you have to do," it whispered, "is let go."

She stared at the outstretched hand, her mind torn between terror and curiosity. The forest, the place that had always been her sanctuary, she now felt, had turned against her. But it was also the only place she had ever truly belonged. She could feel the pull, stronger than ever, the promise of power, of freedom, if only she would surrender to it.

But something deep within her rebelled. A small, fragile part of her—the part that still clung to her humanity—refused to give in. Her hands unclenched, and she took a step back, her heart pounding in her ears.

"No," she said, her voice stronger than she expected.

The figure's eyes narrowed, the shadows around it twisting violently. For the first time, it seemed uncertain.

"No," she repeated, her voice rising. "I'm not yours."

The air shifted, the oppressive weight lifting slightly as if the forest itself hesitated. The figure stood still, its eyes glowing brighter, its form flickering in the moonlight. Then, without a word, it turned and vanished into the darkness, swallowed by the trees.

She stood there, breathing heavily, her body trembling with adrenaline. The forest was silent again, the presence gone, but she knew it wasn't over. It was still out there, waiting, watching.

It had let her go—for now. But the game was far from finished.

Chapter 4: The Last Visit

In the days following her encounter with the figure, she avoided the depths of the forest. She stayed near the edge, where the trees thinned and the sky stretched wide, brushing against the world her siblings had chosen. The world where people lived in houses and spoke in voices loud enough to carry through walls.

It was her father's words that echoed in her mind the most, his gruff warning about the woods: Something old. Something that's been here longer than us. Stay away from it. But her father, like her siblings, had abandoned the forest. They had chosen lives with more structure, beyond the shelter of the trees. They'd tried to take her with them, but her place was in the wild.

Still, a part of her clung to the idea that she could bridge the gap, that maybe she could have both. She remembered where her siblings lived—just beyond the hills, at the edge of the pines, where the woods gave way to small farms and crooked fences. She knew the path.

One evening, as the sun sank below the horizon, she followed the trail to her ol cabin door. The walk was longer than she remembered, each step feeling heavier, her feet dragging through the dirt as if the forest were reluctant to let her go. She could feel the woods behind her, watching, stretching its dark fingers toward her as if trying to pull her back.

When she arrived, her siblings were outside, talking, laughing. She hung back in the shadows, watching for a long time. They looked so different now—clean, dressed in clothes that didn't smell of pine or sweat. They moved with ease, their bodies unburdened by the weight of the woods.

For a moment, she imagined stepping forward, joining them. She imagined sitting at the table, eating the food they'd prepared, feeling their arms around her in warm, familiar embraces.

But when she did step out of the shadows, something shifted. The laughter died, their faces hardening as they turned to look at her. Her brother, Will, took a step forward, his eyes scanning her dirty clothes, her wild hair, her bare feet.

"You're still...out there?" he said quietly, as if speaking too loud would spook her.

She nodded, her eyes flicking between them, searching for any sign that they still saw her as one of them.

"You shouldn't be here," her sister Clara said, her voice tight. "You've been out there too long."

Her heart sank. She opened her mouth to speak, to tell them about the presence, the thing that was out there in the woods, but the words stuck in her throat. They wouldn't understand. How could they? They had chosen to leave the wild behind, to become something else, something that didn't belong to the trees anymore.

Her brother took another step forward, but it wasn't to embrace her. It was to shield her young sister, Evelyn from the view, as though she were dangerous now, a stranger to be kept at a distance.

"Go back," he said softly. "Go back to your woods... they've always been your true home. Not here. Not with us."

She stood there for a long moment, her heart pounding, her mind racing with everything she wanted to say. But there were no words that could bridge the chasm that had grown between them.

Without another word, she turned and disappeared back into the forest.

The walk back to the woods felt heavier than the walk away. The trees closed in around her as she moved deeper, their branches tugging at her hair, their roots curling around her feet as if to claim her once and for all. She could feel the presence again, waiting, watching, as though it had known this would happen.

She stopped at the place where she had first seen the figure. The moon hung low in the sky, casting long shadows across the ground. The air was thick, the oppressive weight of the woods settling over her shoulders like a cloak.

She wasn't afraid anymore. She knew now that there was no going back, no returning to the life her siblings had chosen. The woods were her home. They always had been.

And the presence—whatever it was—had been waiting for her to accept that.

She stepped into the clearing, her feet sinking into the damp earth. "I'm here," she called out, her voice steady. "I'm not leaving. They don't want me anymore."

The silence that followed was thick and heavy, stretching out until it became unbearable. And then, slowly, the shadows began to move. The figure emerged from the darkness, just as it had before, its tall, skeletal form gliding toward her. Its eyes gleamed in the moonlight, brighter than she remembered, burning with a cold, ancient fire.

"You've come back," it said, its voice low and smooth, echoing through the trees.

"I never left," she replied, standing her ground. "Not really."

The figure smiled, a slow, sinister smile that twisted its pale face. "You are not like the others. You never were."

She didn't flinch this time. She met its gaze, her heart steady. "What do you want from me?"

The figure tilted its head, considering her. "I want what is already mine. You."

She took a deep breath, her mind clearer now than it had ever been. "Then take me. I'm here. I'm yours now."

The figure stepped closer, its eyes glowing brighter. "You will become one with the forest. You will become more than human, more than animal. You will be wild—a force of nature, like the wind and the rain. But you will belong to me."

She nodded, the weight of the decision settling over her like a heavy cloak. "I was never meant to leave."

The figure's smile widened. "No. You were meant to stay. And now, you are mine."

As the words left its mouth, the forest around them seemed to come alive. The trees creaked and groaned, their branches twisting toward her, the earth beneath her feet rumbling. The figure extended a hand, its long, claw-like fingers brushing against her skin.

A chill ran through her, but it wasn't fear. It was something else—something deeper. She could feel the power of the woods seeping into her, filling her veins, flooding her senses. The boundaries between her and the forest blurred, the lines between human and wild vanishing.

She closed her eyes, letting the forest claim her, letting the presence take hold.

She was no longer just a girl, no longer just a daughter of the woods. She was something more. Something darker. Something wilder.

And she was never leaving.

Chapter 5: Becoming Wild

The moment she surrendered to the forest, the world shifted. Time, once a steady river of days and nights, became fragmented, and erratic. The passing of seasons no longer mattered; her existence was no longer tethered to human concerns. The wild in her stirred, awakening a primal power that coursed through her blood like the rivers cutting through the Pine Barrens.

Her senses sharpened. She could hear the rustle of leaves miles away, the flutter of a bird's wings, the soft, nearly imperceptible steps of a deer weaving through the underbrush. Her body moved with an animal's grace, instinct guiding her through the maze of trees as if the woods were her true skin, her bones rooted in the very earth she walked.

She easily found fresh water and primal needs to sustain her. She knew instinctively where to find berries, roots, and fiddler heads. She could identify and consume the natural forest flowers, herbs, and mushrooms to sustain her and keep her healthy and strong. It all came natural to her. A plethora of knowledge that somehow was imbedded in her very soul and mind.

The figure—her guide, her master—was never far, though it no longer needed to show itself to her. It was everywhere, in the whispering branches and the flicker of shadows. She could feel its presence deep in her bones, a part of her now. It had made her wild, and with that wildness came power.

But with power came a hunger. A deep, insatiable need that gnawed at her insides. Even as she nourished her body with the bounty of the woods vegetation she had this deep guttural pain of primordial hunger.

At first, it was manageable—a quiet, dull ache. But as the days passed, the hunger grew. It demanded more, something the woods themselves could not give. It wasn't food she craved, nor water. It was something darker, something rooted in the same place as the sinister force that had claimed her.

One night, as she lay beneath a canopy of stars, her heart thrumming with the energy of the wild, she felt it stir—the hunger, the insidious whisper in her mind.

"Feed it," the voice said. "Feed the wild. Feed the forest."

She sat up, her heart racing, her eyes scanning the darkened forest. The trees stood still, but she could feel the presence in the air, heavy and waiting. It wanted something from her. She understood now that her transformation was not the end, but the beginning of something much darker.

She rose to her feet, her muscles tense, and followed the whisper, letting it guide her deeper into the heart of the woods. The air grew colder as she moved, the ground beneath her feet slick with moisture. The shadows grew thicker, the trees towering above her like ancient sentinels. She knew she was nearing the core of the forest, the place where the power that had claimed her was strongest.

It wasn't long before she found it—the source of the whispering, the place where the hunger could be fed.

A small clearing opened before her, and in its center stood a tree unlike any other she had ever seen. Its bark was black as pitch, its branches twisted and gnarled, reaching out like the arms of some ancient, sleeping beast. The air around it crackled with energy, a pulse that matched the beat of her own heart.

She approached the tree cautiously, her steps slow, her eyes wide with wonder and fear. The whispering grew louder, more insistent as if the tree itself was calling to her.

"Feed it," the voice urged again. "Give it what it wants."

She knelt before the tree, her fingers brushing against the cold, rough bark. A shiver ran through her body, and in that moment, she understood what the tree—what the force—wanted. It needed life. Blood. A sacrifice to seal her bond with the forest.

Her mind reeled, but her body moved with a strange, undeniable compulsion. She rose to her feet and scanned the edge of the clearing. The animals had always trusted her, had always come to her without fear. Tonight, one of them would not leave.

It didn't take long for a deer to appear, stepping cautiously into the clearing, its large brown eyes fixed on her. She held its gaze, her breath steady, her pulse calm. The deer moved closer, as if drawn to her by some invisible force, its movements slow, deliberate.

She reached out a hand, and the deer nuzzled her palm, its warm breath brushing against her skin. For a moment, she hesitated, the last fragments of her humanity flickering in her mind. But then the hunger surged, overpowering everything else.

With one swift, brutal motion, she snapped the deer's neck.

The sound of the bones breaking echoed through the clearing, and the deer crumpled to the ground, lifeless. She knelt beside its body, her hands trembling as she pressed them to the ground. The earth beneath her seemed to pulse in response, as if alive, as if feeding on the energy of the sacrifice.

The black tree groaned, its branches creaking as they twisted toward the sky. Its roots moving under ground and across the clearing to where she and the sacrificial deer were on the ground. The air around her shimmered with dark energy, and she could feel the force—the presence—growing stronger, feeding on the life she had given it. Its roots like vines twisting around the animal like a cocoon, tightening, coiling, and breaking its bones. Desalving life and pulling it underground to feed on its very soul.

"You are one with the wild now," the voice whispered, but this time it wasn't just in her head. It was everywhere, carried on the wind, woven into the fabric of the forest. "You are mine. You are ours. We are all one"

She stood, her body thrumming with power, the blood of the deer staining her hands yet as she looked down the blood was somehow dripping and pulling from her skin right into the ground at her feet. She no longer felt any hesitation, no longer questioned what she had done. The hunger had been fed, but she knew it wouldn't be the last time. The wild demanded more, and she was bound to it now, a part of something much larger, much older than herself. Something ancient and malevolent.

As she turned to leave the clearing, the black tree loomed behind her, its twisted branches casting long shadows across the forest floor. The presence followed her, silent now, but ever-watchful, ever-waiting.

She was no longer just a daughter of the woods. She was the wild itself—feral, untamed, and bound to the darkness that had claimed her.

Her descent into the wild had left her completely transformed, more powerful but bound to darker forces.

Chapter 6: The Boundaries of the Wild

The boundaries of the forest became clearer in the days that followed her first sacrifice. The trees seemed to press closer together, hemming her in, as if to remind her of the invisible line she could not cross. Beyond the woods lay the world she had once known—her family, the farms, the roads, and towns that felt like a dream now, distant and unreal.

But the forest was no longer just a home. It was also prison.

The more she wandered, the more the woods closed in around her, thickening, twisting, shaping themselves to keep her from leaving. Paths she had once known became overgrown, impassable. Familiar landmarks shifted, or disappeared altogether. When she strayed too far toward the edges, the presence returned, looming in her mind, urging her back toward the center.

Each night, she felt it more keenly—the gnawing hunger, the pull of the black tree, and the whisper that never left her. It reminded her that her bond with the forest was sealed in blood. She couldn't deny it now. She was a part of something older, darker, and it was ever hungry.

As the days passed, she ventured farther from the black tree but never dared too close to the edge of the woods. Her mind was often drawn back to her family—wondering if they even thought of her anymore. Did her siblings remember the girl she had been, the one they had left behind in the wilderness? Or had they buried her memory along with the wildness they had escaped?

One evening, as the sun dipped below the horizon, casting long shadows through the trees, she found herself near the old road leading out of the woods. The sight of it stirred something in her, a faint, flickering memory of her life before the wild claimed her. She stood still, watching the dark strip of packed earth and gravel stretching out before her, the line between the world she had known and the one that now held her captive.

For a moment, she imagined stepping onto the road, leaving the woods behind, walking to the village, to the farm, to her siblings, to the life she had once imagined for herself.

But before she could take a step, the air shifted around her.

The presence stirred, stronger this time, colder, wrapping itself around her like a creeping fog. She felt it in her bones, a weight pressing against her chest, pulling her back from the edge of the road. Her breath quickened, and for the first time since her transformation, she felt something close to fear.

"I am yours now," she whispered, but the words didn't feel true. It was more like a sadness. She shook her head, "No."

The forest pulsed in response. She could hear the trees creaking, the underbrush rustling, as if the woods themselves were alive with the presence's anger. It wasn't just a force in her mind anymore—it was the woods themselves, growing darker, more dangerous.

A chill ran down her spine as she took a step back from the road, the pull of the forest growing stronger. The presence was angry. It wanted her to stay. It demanded it.

And then, out of the corner of her eye, she saw something move.

A figure stood at the edge of the road, cloaked in shadow. It was tall, its body shrouded in darkness, but its eyes gleamed—two pinpricks of cold, white light. The same eyes she had seen before.

The sinister force had come to her again.

"You cannot leave," the figure whispered, its voice carried on the wind. "You belong to the pines now."

She didn't reply. She couldn't. Her feet were rooted to the ground, her heart pounding in her chest. The hunger she had felt before, the one that had driven her to sacrifice, surged within her again, stronger, more violent.

The figure stepped closer, its eyes burning into her. "Do you wish to challenge your bond?"

She swallowed, her throat dry. She didn't want to challenge it. She wanted to understand it. "Why me?" she asked, her voice barely above a whisper.

The figure stopped, just a few feet from her now. "Because you were always wild," it said, its voice soft, but full of power. "You were always meant to be one with the forest. Your family never understood. They could not. But you... you belong."

She shook her head, her mind racing. "I didn't choose this."

The figure's smile widened, dark and terrible. "No one chooses the pines. The pines choose you."

The weight of those words settled over her, suffocating, pressing down on her chest. She had always thought she could leave, that maybe one day she could walk out of the woods, find her family again, and return to the world. But now she understood the truth. The pine barrens had chosen her long ago, before she had even known its name, before she had ever stepped foot in the woods.

And now it would never let her go.

The figure reached out, its hand hovering inches from her face. "You are bound to this place. You are bound to me, to Us. Do not fight it."

Her breath caught in her throat as she stared into those gleaming eyes. She knew she couldn't fight it. The wild pines and black tree were in her blood now, a part of her very being. But the presence—this force—wasn't just the woods. It was something more. Something ancient. Something hungry.

"I don't want to feed it anymore," she whispered.

The figure's smile faltered, its eyes narrowing. "The wild feeds. It always feeds. In time you will too. We will become as one."

The hunger surged again, twisting in her stomach, clawing at her insides. She doubled over, her body trembling as the force within her demanded more. Another sacrifice. Another life.

But this time, she resisted. She wouldn't kill again. She wouldn't be the forest's pawn. "I won't."

The figure stepped closer, its voice growing colder, darker. "You will feed Us. You have no choice."

She straightened, her breath coming in ragged gasps. "I do," she said, her voice steadier than she felt. "I can resist."

The figure's smile returned, cruel and sharp. "You can try."

And with that, it vanished, dissolving into the shadows, leaving her alone with the trees and the hunger that gnawed at her soul.

She stood there for a long time, staring at the road, the boundary between her two worlds. But now, she knew her true fate. She was bound here.

There was no escape.

She was bound to the wild, bound to the hunger, bound to the sinister force that controlled the woods.

But she wouldn't feed it. Not anymore.

She would find a way to break the bond. Or die trying.

Chapter 7: Defiance in the Dark

The days that followed were a blur of tension and silence. The forest around her seemed to watch, waiting for her to falter, to give in to the hunger that still pulsed deep in her bones. The trees no longer whispered as they once did, and the animals—once so drawn to her—had grown distant. She could feel the forest's displeasure in the way the air turned heavy, thick with something unspeakable.

But she held her ground.

Each night, she felt the hunger rise again, gnawing at her with an urgency that had become nearly unbearable. Her body cried out for the release that only a sacrifice could provide, but her mind, her will, remained firm. She refused to feed the dark force again.

She spent her days pacing the edges of the woods, searching for signs, any clue as to how she might sever the bond between her and the forest. The black tree haunted her dreams, its twisted branches calling to her, reminding her of the life she had taken to appease it. But no matter how far she walked, no matter how deep she wandered into the shadows, the answer eluded her.

One night, as the air grew cold and the stars flickered above like distant flames, she ventured to the clearing where the black tree stood. Its gnarled form loomed in the darkness, a monument to the force that had claimed her. She could feel the hunger rising again, more insistent now, as if the forest itself was growing impatient.

She approached the tree slowly, her breath steady, her hands clenched at her sides. The bark of the tree was cold beneath her fingertips, rough and ancient, and for a moment, she felt the weight of the centuries pressing down on her.

"You will not win," she whispered to the tree, her voice barely audible. "I will not be your puppet."

The forest rustled in response, the trees swaying as if agitated by her defiance. The black tree seemed to pulse with dark energy, its branches creaking like bones shifting in the night.

Then, from the shadows, the figure emerged once more.

It was taller this time, its form more distinct, though still wrapped in the inky blackness of the forest. Its eyes gleamed in the moonlight, two cold pinpricks of light that bore into her soul.

"You test my patience," it said, its voice low and dangerous. "The wild pines are not kind to those who defy it."

She held her ground, meeting its gaze with a steely resolve. "I won't feed you or it anymore."

The figure moved closer, its form shifting like smoke as it circled her. "You cannot resist forever. The hunger will consume you. It always does."

Her heart pounded in her chest, but she refused to let fear take hold. "Maybe," she said, her voice steady. "But I'll die before I let you control me."

The figure stopped in front of her, its face inches from hers. "Do you think you are stronger than the pines? Stronger than the force that has claimed this land for centuries?"

"I think I can fight," she said. "And that's enough."

For a long moment, the figure said nothing, its gaze locked on hers. Then, slowly, a smile spread across its shadowy face—cold, cruel, and full of something dark.

"Very well," it said, its voice soft but dripping with malice. "You wish to defy me? Then we shall see how strong you truly are."

Before she could react, the figure vanished, dissolving into the shadows once more. The air around her grew colder, the wind picking up, howling through the trees. She turned in a circle, her eyes scanning the darkness, but the figure was gone.

And yet, the presence was stronger than ever.

The ground beneath her feet began to tremble, the earth shifting as the black tree groaned and twisted. Its branches stretched higher, reaching toward the sky as if grasping for something beyond the stars. The air crackled with dark energy, and she could feel the hunger rising again—stronger, more violent, more desperate.

She stumbled back from the tree, her heart racing, her mind reeling. The force was angry now, enraged by her defiance, and it would not be satisfied until it had broken her.

But she would not give in.

She turned and ran, her feet pounding against the forest floor as she fled from the clearing. The trees closed in around her, their branches reaching out like twisted fingers, trying to catch her, to drag her back to the black tree. The wind howled in her ears, and the presence followed her, pressing in on her from all sides.

But she kept running, her breath coming in ragged gasps, her legs burning with the effort. She wouldn't stop. She couldn't stop. Not until she was free.

The woods became a blur around her, the trees and shadows blending into one, but still, she pushed forward. The hunger gnawed at her insides, threatening to tear her apart from the inside out, but she refused to let it win.

Finally, after what felt like hours, she stumbled into a small, secluded grove, the air suddenly still, the presence gone. She collapsed to the ground, her body trembling, her chest heaving as she struggled to catch her breath.

For a moment, there was silence. The wind had died down, and the trees no longer reached for her. It was as if the forest itself had retreated, leaving her alone in the quiet of the night.

She lay there, staring up at the stars, her mind racing. She had escaped the black tree's pull, but the force was still there, lurking in the shadows, waiting for her to falter.

But she wouldn't. She couldn't.

The wild had chosen her, yes, but she would not be its slave. She would find a way to break the bond, no matter the cost.

And if the force wanted a fight, she was ready.

Chapter 8: Shadows of the Past

The quiet of the grove provided a brief respite, but she knew it wouldn't last. The presence was always there, lurking just beyond the trees, waiting for her to make a mistake. But for now, the stars above seemed brighter, their light a faint comfort against the encroaching darkness.

As her breath slowed and her pulse steadied, her thoughts drifted back to her family. They were out there, living in the rural community beyond the woods, a world she had once been part of but could no longer reach. The memory of her siblings tugged at her, stirring something deep within—longing, regret, and a sharp pang of loneliness.

What would they think of her now? Would they even recognize her, this wild, mud-caked creature that the forest had shaped? Or had they forgotten her altogether, left her behind just as they had left the woods?

The thought gnawed at her, even more painfully than the hunger. She had to know. She had to see them, to try, one last time, to reconnect with the life she had lost. Perhaps, if they saw her, they would understand. Perhaps, if they saw what she had become, they would help her break free.

The decision was made before she realized it. She would return to them—if only for a moment—before the forest could pull her back.

Under the cover of night, she moved through the trees, her steps light and quick, her senses heightened as she navigated the forest. The presence seemed to sense her intent, stirring again at the edges of her consciousness, but she pushed it back. The black tree's power flickered, but she refused to let it take hold. She would see her family, and nothing would stop her.

By the time she reached the outskirts of the woods, dawn was breaking, the first light of morning casting a pale glow over the fields that stretched beyond the trees. In the distance, she could see the outline of her childhood home, a small farmhouse nestled among the crops. It seemed so different now, so far removed from the life she had come to know.

Her heart raced as she approached the house, her mind flooded with memories— of laughter, of games played in the fields, of her siblings running through the tall grass with her. She had been part of this world once, before the wild claimed her.

She reached the edge of the field and hesitated, her eyes fixed on the farmhouse. Smoke curled from the chimney, and the faint sound of voices reached her ears. Her family. They were inside, living their lives, unaware of the creature watching them from the edge of the woods.

She took a deep breath and stepped forward.

But before she could take another step, something caught her eye.

A figure stood in the doorway of the farmhouse, watching her. It was her sister, Evelyn, the one just older than herself—older now, taller, her hair pulled back, her face set in a look of confusion and caution. For a moment, they locked eyes across the field, and the world seemed to stop.

Her heart leaped in her chest. She wanted to call out, to say something, anything, to bridge the gap between them. But the words wouldn't come. Instead, she stood frozen, the distance between them suddenly insurmountable.

Her sister took a step forward, her expression softening as recognition flickered in her eyes. But then, as if sensing something wrong, she stopped. Her gaze shifted to the woods behind her, and a shadow passed over her face.

The presence surged again, strong and angry, wrapping itself around her like a tightening noose. The forest was pulling her back, furious that she had dared to stray so far.

She clenched her fists, fighting the urge to turn and run. But the pull was too strong, the hunger too powerful. The wild was calling her home.

With one last, desperate glance at her sister, she turned and fled back into the woods, her heart breaking as the distance between them grew.

She didn't stop running until she was deep within the forest, the black tree looming before her once again. Her chest heaved with exhaustion, tears burning in her eyes, but she refused to let them fall.

The figure was there, waiting for her.

"You see now," it said, its voice cold and triumphant. "You cannot return. You do not belong with them anymore."

She wiped her eyes, anger rising in her chest. "You don't control me."

The figure stepped closer, its eyes gleaming in the darkness. "But I do. You are bound to this place, bound to me. You cannot escape the pines."

"I will find a way," she said through gritted teeth. "I will break this bond."

The figure's smile was cruel, mocking. "You are welcome to try. But the pines always win. It is in your blood now. You belong to Us."

She stepped back, her breath ragged, her mind racing. The weight of the forest pressed down on her, the hunger clawing at her insides, but she refused to give in.

She had seen her family again, if only for a moment. And that moment was enough to remind her of who she used to be, of the life she had once lived.

She wasn't just a creature of the woods. She wasn't just a pawn in the forest's game.

She was still herself. And she would fight to reclaim her humanity.

Turning her back on the black tree and the figure, she walked deeper into the woods, her resolve hardening with each step. There had to be a way to break free, to sever the bond that held her captive.

And she would find it.

No matter the cost.

Chapter 9: The Edge of Madness

The deeper she went, the darker the woods became. The trees twisted and gnarled, their branches like skeletal fingers clawing at the sky. The air grew thick and cold, suffocating in its weight, and the usual hum of the forest was replaced by a deafening silence. Even the animals—those that had once circled her in reverence—were gone, hiding in the shadows as though they sensed what was coming.

She could feel the black tree's influence spreading like poison through her veins. Every step she took felt heavier, as though the forest itself was trying to pull her under, to drag her into the earth and consume her whole. But she kept moving, driven by something darker, something more dangerous than fear.

Rage.

It bubbled up inside her, wild and uncontrollable, feeding off the hunger that gnawed at her from within. The presence, the figure—it had stolen everything from her. Her family, her freedom, even her mind. It had made her into something she no longer recognized, something feral and broken. But it had also underestimated her.

She would not be its puppet.

As she walked, her eyes flickered with an intensity she hadn't felt before. The ground beneath her trembled, the trees groaning as if in pain, but she didn't falter. She was done running. She was done being afraid.

The black tree stood in the distance now, its branches like twisted veins against the sky. She could feel its pull, stronger than ever, calling her back to it. But this time, she wasn't coming to submit.

She was coming to destroy it.

The figure appeared before her, rising from the shadows like smoke. Its form was more distinct now, more human, though its face was still a blur of darkness. Its eyes, however, glowed with cold, sharp light, and when it spoke, its voice was a hiss of fury.

"You are foolish to defy me," it said, circling her slowly, its presence filling the air with dread. "The pines are in your blood. You cannot escape Us."

"I don't want to escape," she replied, her voice low and steady. "I want to end this."

The figure paused, its eyes narrowing. "End this?" It let out a dark, mocking laugh. "You cannot end what is eternal. The pines have claimed you. You are bound to it as I am."

She clenched her fists, her nails digging into her palms until they bled. "I never agreed to this. You took me. You made me into this."

"I showed you the truth," the figure said, its voice softening into something almost seductive. "The pines are freedom. No rules. No chains. You belong here, with me, with Us, where no one can hurt you again."

For a moment, the hunger flared inside her, urging her to give in, to submit, to let the dark power consume her. But then she thought of her family, of the fleeting glimpse of her sister standing in the doorway, and the hunger twisted into something else—hatred.

"I'd rather die," she said through gritted teeth.

The figure's eyes flared with rage, and the ground beneath her feet cracked, splitting open as the forest seemed to roar in anger. The black tree's branches stretched toward her, hungry, eager to claim her once more.

But she didn't back down.

She stepped forward, toward the tree, her breath coming in shallow bursts as the air grew thick with dark energy. The figure lunged at her, its shadowy hands outstretched, but she ducked beneath its grasp and kept moving, her eyes locked on the tree.

The closer she got, the more the hunger tore at her, threatening to rip her apart from the inside. The black tree pulsed with malevolent energy, its bark writhing as though alive, and the ground trembled beneath it. The force was stronger now, desperate to consume her, to break her will once and for all.

But she was done being afraid.

She reached the base of the tree, her hand trembling as she placed it on the rough, cold bark. The darkness surged through her, violent and all-consuming, but she didn't pull away. Instead, she pushed back, using the rage, the hatred, to fuel her.

"I am not yours," she whispered, her voice trembling with fury. "You don't own me."

The tree shuddered beneath her touch, the dark energy rippling through the air like a storm about to break. The figure appeared again, standing just behind her, its voice a hiss in her ear.

"You cannot destroy what you are. The pines are you."

She turned, her eyes burning with defiance. "Then I'll destroy myself."

Before the figure could react, she drove her hand deeper into the tree's bark, feeling it give way beneath her touch. The black energy surged through her, violent and chaotic, but she welcomed it now, let it wash over her, let it tear at her mind and body.

The figure screamed, its form flickering as the forest around them seemed to collapse inward. The trees twisted and groaned, their branches snapping like bones, the ground splitting open as dark tendrils of energy writhed up from the earth. The sky above turned black, the stars disappearing as the presence consumed everything in its path.

But she didn't stop.

She shoved her other hand into the tree, feeling its ancient, corrupted power coursing through her veins. The hunger inside her reached its peak, and for a moment, she felt as though she might be swallowed whole by the darkness.

But then she heard it—a voice, faint and distant, but unmistakable.

Her sister's voice.

She wasn't sure if it was real or just a fragment of memory, but it gave her strength. She could hear her name, whispered in the wind, a reminder that she was more than just a creature of the wild. She was still human. She was still herself.

With a scream of pure defiance, she ripped her hands from the tree, tearing it apart with all the strength she had left. Tearing and clawing at its bark and branches. The black energy exploded outward, a wave of darkness that rippled through the forest, shattering the trees, splitting the ground, and sending the figure spiraling into the void.

The force that had bound her to the wild, that had claimed her as its own, was gone.

The forest fell silent.

She collapsed to the ground, her body trembling, her breath ragged. The hunger was still there, but it was weaker now, a shadow of what it once was. She had broken the bond, severed the connection.

But as she lay there, staring up at the sky, she knew the pines would never truly leave her. It was a part of her now, buried deep, waiting to resurface. She had won this small battle, but the war was far from over.

And as the dark clouds began to gather once more, she knew the forest wasn't finished with her yet.

Chapter 10: The Forest Watches

She lay motionless on the cold, damp earth, her breath shallow and her limbs heavy as if the very act of tearing the black tree apart had drained her of everything. The sky above her was still shrouded in thick, swirling clouds, but there was no movement in the forest, no sound save for the distant rustle of leaves in the wind. It felt like the woods were holding their breath, waiting, watching.

Her body ached, the weight of exhaustion pressing her deeper into the ground, but she couldn't rest. Not yet. She had broken the tree, destroyed the presence that had enslaved her, but the wild still coursed through her veins. The power, though weakened, was still there, lurking beneath her skin like a beast waiting to pounce.

She forced herself to sit up, her vision blurry as she glanced around. The clearing where the black tree had stood was now a crater of splintered wood and broken earth, the once towering structure reduced to fragments. The dark energy that had surrounded it was gone, dissipated into the air, but the forest felt no less dangerous. If anything, it felt more hostile, more aware of her presence.

She had defied the pines. And the woods did not forget.

With trembling hands, she pushed herself to her feet, her legs barely holding her as she staggered away from the shattered remains of the tree. The air was thick with tension, the ground beneath her feet soft and unstable, as though the forest was shifting, changing around her.

She was alone, but she could feel the eyes of the woods on her. The presence she had fought wasn't just a force—it was the forest itself. And though she had broken free, she had not won. Not truly. The wild would always be part of her, a shadow in her soul, a whisper in the back of her mind.

As she stumbled through the trees, her body protesting with every step, she thought of her family again. The fleeting glimpse of her sister at the farmhouse, the look of confusion and fear in her eyes. She had gone there to reconnect, to remind herself of the life she had once had, but now it seemed farther away than ever.

She could never return. The pines wouldn't let her.

The realization hit her like a punch to the chest, and she stopped, her hands gripping the nearest tree for support. Her breath came in ragged gasps, her heart pounding in her ears. She had always known, deep down, that this was her fate, that the forest would never let her go. But she had clung to hope, to the idea that she might find a way out, that she could reclaim some part of herself.

That hope was gone now, swallowed by the dark.

She wasn't human anymore. Not really. She had become something else, something more primal, more dangerous. And as much as she now hated the pines, she couldn't deny that it was part of her, perhaps it always had been.

She closed her eyes, her fingers digging into the rough bark of the tree. The presence was gone, the force that had controlled her broken, but she could still feel the pulse of the forest beneath her skin. It whispered to her, in a language older than words, promising power, freedom, and something darker.

The hunger flared again, sharper this time, more insistent. It gnawed at her, a constant reminder that the wild was still in control.

"I won't let you take me," she whispered, though her voice was hoarse and filled with doubt. She was weak and struggling for breath. Her eyes weakened and rolled back. Her body began to tremble, not from fear but from a deep emptiness that had overtaken her body, her physical being.

The forest didn't respond. It didn't need to. It had already won.

She pushed away from the tree and kept moving, her steps slow and unsteady. The deeper she went, the darker the woods became, the shadows stretching long and sharp across the ground. The trees seemed to close in around her, their branches reaching for her like skeletal hands.

She didn't know where she was going, only that she had to keep moving, keep running. The darkness was still inside her, but she wouldn't let it consume her completely. Not yet.

But as the hours passed and the sky above grew darker, she began to feel it again—the presence. Not the figure she had fought before, but something else. Something deeper. It moved through the trees, unseen but felt, like a shadow too thick to belong to the natural world.

It was watching her. Waiting.

She stopped, her breath catching in her throat, her body tensing. The air around her was thick with anticipation, the silence deafening. She could feel it now, closer than before, as though it had always been there, lurking just beyond the edges of her awareness.

A cold wind brushed past her, sending a shiver down her spine. The trees groaned, their branches creaking ominously, and the ground beneath her feet seemed to shift.

The forest was alive. And it was angry.

Suddenly, the shadows around her twisted, warping into unnatural shapes. They moved, slithering across the ground like serpents, encircling her, closing in.

Her heart raced as she backed away, her eyes wide with terror. The presence was stronger now, more tangible, as though it had taken form. She could feel it pressing down on her, suffocating her with its weight.

This wasn't just the woods. This was something far older, far darker.

And it wanted her. It was not going to let her go.

She turned and ran, her feet pounding against the soft earth as the shadows followed, stretching out in pursuit. The forest blurred around her, the trees bending and twisting as though they were alive, reaching out to trap her, to pull her back in.

The presence was everywhere, all-encompassing, filling the air with its malevolent force. It was no longer just a part of the forest. It was the forest. And it was hunting her.

She could feel its cold breath on her neck, its fingers brushing against her skin as she ran, faster and faster, her lungs burning with the effort. But no matter how fast she went, it was always there, closing in, drawing her deeper into the darkness.

Her legs gave out beneath her, and she fell hard to the ground, her body shaking with exhaustion. The shadows swirled around her, thick and heavy, blotting out the sky.

She was trapped.

The presence moved closer, its form solidifying in the darkness. It loomed over her, its eyes glowing with a cold, ancient light. It was no longer the figure from before. This was something more primal, more powerful. It was the embodiment of the pines, the forest itself made flesh.

And it had come to claim her.

Chapter 11: Fractured Bonds

The farmhouse had grown quieter over the years, the once lively chatter of children replaced by an oppressive silence that hung over the family like a storm cloud. The memories of their time in the woods, of the wild and untamed life they had once embraced, seemed like fragments of a long-lost dream—beautiful in some ways, but laced with a fear that gnawed at them. For the older siblings, leaving the forest had been a choice, a necessity to save their minds and souls from the creeping madness that had begun to take hold.

Their eldest brother, Jack, had been the first to leave. He had always been the one who seemed most grounded, most capable of shouldering the weight of the family's isolation. But even Jack had his breaking point. One late autumn night, after weeks of restless sleep and a growing sense that the trees were watching him, he had packed a small bag and left without a word. He had never looked back, not even when their father cursed his name for abandoning them. Jack's absence was felt keenly, but the rest of them stayed, at least for a time, trying to cling to some sense of normalcy in the only life they had ever known.

Then, one by one, the others had followed.

Their brother Will had gone too. Always the dreamer, he had lingered longer than the others, caught between the pull of the woods and the desire to see the world beyond. But Will's dreams had turned into nightmares. He had seen things in the forest, glimpses of shadows that moved too quickly, of eyes that glowed in the dark, watching him. One morning, after yet another night spent staring out the window with bloodshot eyes, he had announced that he was leaving for good. "This place is cursed," he'd muttered as he slung his bag over his shoulder. "It'll eat us alive if we stay."

And then there was a younger sister, the last to leave after the feral daughter's final descent into the wild. She had tried so hard to stay, to hold the family together, but the weight of it all had been too much for her fragile heart. She had loved her feral sister deeply, perhaps more than the others, and her departure had been the hardest of all. She had gone into the woods time and time again, calling her sister's name, leaving offerings of food and clothing at the edge of the clearing. But each time, the woods had refused to give her back. And when their father had forbidden her from venturing into the trees again, she had left. The silence in the house after Clara was gone was unbearable.

Now, only the father and Evelyn, the sister who had remained stood against the growing darkness. The house, once filled with the sounds of life, had become a tomb of memories. The father had grown thin and gaunt, his once powerful frame diminished by the years of isolation and loss. His eyes were hollow, his face lined with bitterness and regret. He seldom spoke, and when he did, it was often to mutter curses about the woods, about the pines that had taken his family. Had taken his wife.

The mother of these cursed children was never quite the same after her daughter disappeared into the shadows of the forest, a haunting echo of laughter and wildness left behind in the empty spaces of their home. She would wander through the house late at night, whispering her daughter's name as if the girl might emerge from a dark corner or shadow. She kept the child's room untouched, clinging to the hope that one day she'd return, wild and strange as she was. But as months stretched into years, that hope became something hollow, something sharp, piercing deeper with every passing day.

Grief transformed into a desperate obsession, and the mother could feel the walls of the house closing in on her, their silence unbearable. She took to the woods, searching, calling out into the darkness for her lost child, hearing only the wind in return. The whispers and strange calls of the forest fed her madness, and she began to believe the tales that her daughter had become something unnatural, something bound to the Barrens forever. The weight of it all—her guilt, her sorrow, her unanswered questions—grew heavier until, in the end, she could no longer bear it. Broken by grief and haunted by the spirit of her daughter in the woods, she took her own life, surrendering herself to the darkness that had claimed her child.

For the sister who remained, the dread was a constant companion. Every creak of the house, every gust of wind through the trees, sent a shiver down her spine. Evelyn tried to maintain some semblance of hope, telling herself that her feral sister would return one day, that she would come back to them whole and human. But as the days dragged on, that hope withered, replaced by a growing sense of dread.

She couldn't forget the look in her sister's eyes the last time she had seen her—the wild, animalistic light that had flickered there, the way she had moved like a beast, wary and silent. She had wanted to run to her, to pull her back, but the fear had held her still. And then her sister had turned and disappeared into the shadows, and Evelyn had known, deep down, that she might never see her again.

The eldest brother, Jack, sat on the edge of a small town, miles from the forest, trying to build a life far removed from the shadow of the woods. He had found work on a farm, laboring in the fields, his hands rough and calloused from years of hard toil. But even here, far from the Pine Barrens, he couldn't shake the memories of the forest. At night, when the wind howled through the fields, it sounded too much like the wind that had once whispered through the trees. He would lie awake, his mind drifting back to the day he had left, to the sound of the wild calling after him.

He tried not to think of his sister—Evelyn-the one they had left behind. But she haunted him, just as the woods haunted him. The guilt gnawed at him, a constant reminder that he had abandoned her, left her to the wilds that had already begun to claim her. He had never spoken of her to anyone in town, never told them about his feral girl who had once been his sister. It was too painful, too strange to explain.

Sam, too, had settled in a small town on the outskirts of civilization, far from the reaches of the Pine Barrens. He had found solace in books, in stories of other worlds, other places where the pines didn't press in on all sides. But no matter how far he ran, the memories followed. Sometimes, in the quiet of the evening, he would imagine he could hear his sister's voice calling to him from the trees, distant and full of longing. But he knew it was just his mind playing tricks on him. She was lost to them now. Lost to the world. To humanity.

Back at the farmhouse, Evelyn had stayed and felt the weight of their absence like a physical thing. Each sibling had left the woods behind, but none of them had truly escaped. The wild had marked them, leaving invisible scars that would never fully heal. And now, as she stood by the window, staring out into the trees, she wondered if the same fate awaited her. Would the woods take her, too, as it had taken their sister? Or was she already lost, trapped in this place, waiting for the darkness to claim her as well?

Her father shuffled past her, his eyes dull and lifeless. He had given up long ago, resigned to the knowledge that the woods had won. But she wasn't ready to give up. Not yet. She had to believe that there was still a way to bring her sister back, to break the hold the pines had on her. But as the wind howled through the trees, carrying with it the eerie, mournful sound of the forest, she wasn't sure anymore.

Something had shifted in the woods. Something darker, more malevolent. And it was coming for them all.

Chapter 12: The Embrace of Shadows

The air in the forest was thick with a weight that pressed down on her like invisible hands, guiding her deeper into its heart. The feral daughter moved with the grace of an animal, her feet light against the earth, her senses sharpened to the sounds around her—the rustle of leaves, the distant calls of birds, the soft hum of the wind as it whispered through the trees. But beneath the familiar sounds of the wood, there was something else—something darker, more insidious, that thrummed beneath the surface. It was like a heartbeat, slow and patient, waiting for her.

For years, she had known only the forest. Its rhythms were her rhythms, its silence her silence. The animals had become her companions, their movements and sounds a language she understood more deeply than human speech. She had long stopped remembering the world beyond the trees, beyond the thick canopy that shielded her from the harshness of human eyes.

But lately, the forest felt different. There was an unease that had taken root, a sense that something was watching her, waiting just beyond the edge of her awareness. At first, she had tried to ignore it, telling herself it was nothing more than the natural pulse of the wild. But it had grown stronger, more persistent, until it was a constant presence that she could no longer escape.

The darkness had begun to feel like a part of her.

The shadows between the trees seemed to stretch longer now, reaching out to her like fingers, brushing against her skin. Sometimes, in the deepest parts of the night, she would feel something stir in the distance, a presence that sent a chill through her body. It wasn't just an animal stalking its prey—this was something else. Something old. She could feel it in her bones.

The forest had always been alive to her, but this... this was different. This was a hunger, a malevolence that wrapped around her like a fog. She no longer feared the beasts that roamed the woods at night—the wolves, the coyotes, the silent birds of prey that hunted in the shadows. They were her kin. Her brethren. But this presence... it was not of the forest. It was deeper, more primal. It was ancient and it stalked her.

There were nights when she would sit by the edge of the stream, her reflection fractured in the rippling water, and she would swear she saw something else staring back at her. Not the wild girl she had become, but something darker, something with hollow eyes and sharp, jagged teeth. The face would shift, and in that brief moment, she would feel it—a pulse of energy that made the air crackle around her, as though the very fabric of the world was being torn open, just for a heartbeat.

She had tried, once, to leave. To find her way back to her family.

She had ventured beyond the trees, following the vague memories of the farmhouse, of her siblings, of the life she had once known. But the moment she stepped beyond the treeline, the world shifted beneath her feet. The earth felt wrong, unnatural, like stepping into a place where she didn't belong. The sky above seemed too bright, too empty, as if it were mocking her for even thinking she could return. The feeling of something pulling her back into the woods was undeniable, a force too strong to resist.

Her body rebelled, her heart racing with a primal fear. She had turned, not out of choice, but because it felt as though the woods were calling her back. As if it was the only place she could ever truly exist.

The world outside the pines was no longer hers.

In the farmhouse, the silence between her father and Evelyn was thick with unspoken dread. They both felt it—the growing weight of the darkness in the woods. It was no longer just the fear of losing her—it was the knowledge that something far more sinister was pulling her away, deeper into the woods. They had heard the stories, the whispered legends of ancient forces that lurked in the Pine Barrens, forces that preyed on the lost, on the vulnerable. But none of them had believed it—until now.

The sister who had stayed clutched the blanket tighter around her shoulders as she sat by the window, staring out into the shadowed woods. Her eyes, once filled with hope, were now clouded with fear. She couldn't shake the feeling that her feral sister was no longer alone out there, that something else had claimed her, twisted her into something unrecognizable.

"She's gone, you know that," her father's voice cracked the silence, his tone bitter, broken. His face was gaunt, hollowed by years of grief and anger. "There's no saving her. She's part of that place now. Part of the darkness."

The words hung in the air like a curse.

But Evelyn refused to believe it. Not entirely. She still felt a connection, a thread between them, though it was fraying. She couldn't explain it, but she knew her sister was still out there, somewhere in the dark. She wasn't ready to give up. But each day that passed, the pull of the forest grew stronger. Sometimes, in the dead of night, she would hear her sister's voice in the wind, faint and distant, calling her name. But when she ventured to the edge of the woods, all she found was silence.

Deep down, she knew something was changing in the woods. It wasn't just her sister who was slipping away—it was the forest itself. The trees seemed to shift, their shadows growing darker, deeper. The air felt heavier, the atmosphere charged with an energy that made her skin crawl. She could feel it watching her too, whatever it was.

The feral daughter moved through the woods as though she were a part of it, her body blending into the shadows, her movements fluid and silent. But the presence followed her, always just out of sight. She could feel its eyes on her, cold and unforgiving. And yet, there was a strange comfort in it, a familiarity. It was as if the darkness had become her constant companion, and in its embrace, she found a twisted sense of belonging.

She had stopped trying to resist it.

The wild had claimed her long ago, and now, the darkness was finishing what it had started.

She could feel the presence growing stronger with each passing day, its pull undeniable. And deep inside, she knew that a confrontation was coming. Whatever this force was, it wasn't going to let her go—not until it had consumed her completely.

The shadows whispered to her, beckoning her deeper into the heart of the woods, where the ancient force lay waiting. There, in the place where the trees grew tallest and the air was thick with decay, she would find it. The thing that had been watching her, waiting for her. The thing that had been calling her name.

And when she finally stood before it, she would have to face the truth:

The darkness wasn't just in the woods.

It was in her.

Chapter 13: The Savage Bond

The darkness didn't speak in words. It didn't need to. Its voice was everywhere—in the rustle of leaves, the snap of twigs, the deep, endless silence between the sounds of the forest. It spoke through the chill that sank into her bones when she wandered too deep, through the sudden stillness that filled the air when it was near. The feral daughter could feel it now more than ever, pulsing like a second heartbeat inside her chest, sinking its roots into her mind.

At first, she had resisted it. She had clung to the fleeting memories of her family, of her siblings' laughter and her mother's soft hands. But those memories had faded, blurring into the background of her mind like distant stars swallowed by a black sky. The forest had always been her home, but now, the darkness was something more. It was inescapable, intoxicating. It was pulling her deeper into a savage bond she no longer knew how to escape—or if she even wanted to.

She had become something wild, something almost demon-like.

In the quiet moments, when the moon hung low over the canopy, casting long shadows on the forest floor, she would sit by the ancient oak in the heart of the woods and listen. The darkness whispered to her here, where the ground was soft and wet, covered in decaying leaves and old bones. It spoke in thoughts, not in sounds. It showed her flashes of things she couldn't fully understand—visions of the forest long before she was born, of creatures older than memory that had once roamed these woods. It showed her herself, but not as she had been. No, it showed her as she was now: a part of the forest, a creature of the wood.

Her skin, once pale and smooth, was now marked with scratches and dirt, her hair tangled with leaves and twigs. Her eyes had grown sharper, more animalistic. She could see in the dark now, hear the softest footfalls of prey long before they approached. Her movements were no longer awkward or hesitant; they were fluid, instinctual, as though the very earth beneath her feet was guiding her.

And then there were the dreams.

Each night, as she closed her eyes, the darkness would come for her. At first, it was subtle, creeping into her thoughts like a slow tide. But as time passed, it became more aggressive, filling her dreams with visions of twisted faces and shadowy figures, their eyes glowing red in the gloom. They surrounded her, whispering in a language she didn't understand but somehow knew. They showed her flashes of violence, of teeth and claws, of blood on the ground and the sensation of power coursing through her veins.

The visions were overwhelming, consuming, until one night, she woke up with her hands stained with dirt and blood. She didn't remember where she had been, what she had done. All she knew was that something inside her had shifted. The bond was no longer just a pull—it was a part of her now, woven into the very fabric of her being.

In the world outside the woods, her family continued to feel the weight of her absence like a suffocating fog. The older siblings who had left tried to forget her, tried to convince themselves that she had become lost to them, more animal than human. But there was no escaping the dread that gnawed at them in the quiet hours of the night, no forgetting the fear that she was still out there—wilder, darker, something else entirely.

They never spoke of it directly, but in the eyes of their father and younger sister, they saw the same fear reflected back at them. The same unspoken truth: something had changed in the woods, and it wasn't just her.

The younger sister, Evelyn, clung to hope. She believed her feral sister was still in there, somewhere beneath the dirt and wildness. But each time she ventured near the edge of the forest, she felt the same oppressive weight bearing down on her, the same suffocating sense that something was watching, waiting. The trees seemed to lean in closer, their branches twisted and gnarled like claws, as if the forest itself had become a living thing, eager to swallow her whole.

She had heard the stories—the whispered legends of the Pine Barrens. The tales of things that lived in the shadows, of forces older than man that claimed the lost souls who wandered too far into the woods. But she had never believed them. Not until now. Not until the darkness began to creep into her dreams as well.

The feral daughter was no longer alone. The darkness was with her always now, wrapping around her like a second skin. It wasn't just a force outside of her anymore; it was a part of her, twisting her thoughts, warping her sense of reality. Her eyes were hollow, her skin pale and gaunt. The sharpness in her gaze wasn't human anymore—it was something else, something darker. Something primal.

She didn't feel fear anymore, only the savage thrill that came with the bond she had formed. The darkness had given her strength, had shown her how to move silently through the trees, how to hunt without hesitation. It had whispered secrets to her, things she had never known, things no human should know. And in return, it demanded her loyalty, her obedience.

There were times when she questioned it, when a flicker of her old self would surface, trying to fight against the growing tide of darkness that threatened to consume her completely. But the darkness was patient, relentless. It had waited centuries, it could wait longer. It knew that, in the end, she would eventually belong to it fully.

She could feel it now, more than ever, as the days grew shorter and the nights stretched longer. The bond between them had tightened, its grip suffocating but strangely comforting. It was like a twisted love, a bond forged not out of affection, but out of need, out of a shared hunger for power, for control.

The more she gave in, the more the darkness rewarded her. Her senses sharpened, her mind clearer, her body stronger. But with each gift, the darkness took something in return—a piece of her humanity, a fragment of her soul. She had started to forget the faces of her family, the sound of their voices, the feeling of warmth and love. Those things belonged to another life, a life she no longer wanted.

She was something else now, something stronger, something darker.

And the darkness was waiting for her to fully embrace it.

Chapter 14: You Belong to Me

"You belong to me. You belong to Us. And you always will."

The words came again, soft and seductive, like the rustling of leaves caught in the night wind. They echoed through the hollow of her mind, filling the spaces where thoughts of her family once resided. Each time she heard them, the grip of the forest, of the darkness, tightened around her, and it became harder to remember what was real and what was imagined.

She was crouched low, her fingers digging into the damp earth beneath her. The scent of decay, rich and metallic, filled her nostrils as she listened, waiting for the voice to speak again. The moon hung heavy and full above, casting long shadows across the twisted landscape of the Pine Barrens. Somewhere in the distance, an owl hooted, its call low and mournful, but she barely registered it. Her senses were focused elsewhere—on the whisper that seemed to rise from the very soil, curling around her like a cold breath.

"You belong to me."

The feral daughter closed her eyes, pressing her palms deeper into the ground. The earth was cool against her skin, grounding her in the present, but only just. She could feel the pull now, more than ever, a magnetic force deep within the woods, drawing her closer. The darkness was no longer just a shadow or a whisper. It had form. It had presence. And it wanted her.

She thought of her siblings again—those who had escaped, who had chosen the world of men over the world of beasts. They had always looked at her with fear in their eyes, hadn't they? Even when they were children, they had sensed it. The wildness in her, the strange connection she had to the woods. They had run from it, from her. But she had stayed. She had always belonged here, even before she understood why.

Her older brother had been the first to leave. His departure had been sudden, almost impulsive, as though he couldn't bear another day in the oppressive quiet of the forest. Evelyn remembered the way he had looked at her before he went, his eyes wide and uncertain, as though he was seeing her for the first time. He hadn't said goodbye. None of them had. They had all left in silence, as though speaking aloud would summon the very thing they feared.

But Evelyn had lingered. She had stayed on the edge of the forest, waiting, hoping. Her eyes had been full of tears the last time the feral daughter had seen her, standing just beyond the tree line, calling her name in a voice thick with desperation.

But she hadn't answered. She couldn't. Something had stopped her, something deeper than fear. The darkness had already begun to claim her then, pulling her away from the warmth of her family and into its cold embrace.

"Do you think they'll come for you?" the voice whispered now, its tone almost mocking. "Do you think they'll save you from what you are?"

She shuddered, the muscles in her shoulders tensing as the words burrowed deeper into her mind. No, they wouldn't come for her. Her siblings. Her old fame. They couldn't. They had run. They had left her behind, just as she had left them. There was no salvation, no reunion, no going back.

"You're mine now. You've always been mine."

The words sent a jolt of electricity down her spine. She opened her eyes, her breath coming in ragged bursts as she felt the truth of them. The forest had always owned her. She had known it from the moment she first wandered into the heart of the Pine Barrens as a child, her feet bare and dirty, her heart racing with the thrill of being alone in the wild. The trees had whispered to her then, just as they did now, and she had listened. She had let them guide her deeper, into the darkness, into the unknown.

She rose to her feet slowly, her legs shaky beneath her. The darkness stirred around her, its presence stronger now, as though sensing her surrender. The pull was irresistible. The savage bond between them had grown tighter, thicker, until it felt like a physical thing, a tether that connected her to the very roots of the forest.

"You belong to me."

The words came again, louder this time, more insistent.

And this time, she didn't resist.

She took a step forward, her body moving as though guided by an invisible hand. The air was thick with the scent of moss and rot, the sounds of the forest muted beneath the thrumming in her chest. Her heartbeat matched the rhythm of the woods now, slow and steady, in sync with the ancient force that called to her. She could feel it in the ground beneath her feet, in the wind that brushed against her skin. It was everywhere, surrounding her, filling her.

Her family was gone. They had chosen to leave the forest, and in doing so, they had severed whatever fragile connection had remained between them. She had tried, once, to find her way back to them. But the darkness had shown her the truth. She didn't belong with them. She never had.

The bond was complete now. She was the forest, and the forest was her.

With each step, she felt herself slipping further from the girl she had once been, from the child who had played in the trees with her siblings, who had laughed and danced in the sunlight. That girl was gone, swallowed by the shadows, consumed by the darkness. In her place was something new, something dark and untamed, something that belonged to the wild and nothing else.

As she reached the heart of the woods, the ancient oak loomed before her, its twisted branches reaching up toward the night sky like claws. The air was colder here, the shadows darker, deeper. She knelt at the base of the tree, her hands resting on the rough bark, her head bowed.

The darkness pulsed around her, its presence almost tangible, wrapping around her like a cloak. She closed her eyes, letting it wash over her, letting it take her.

"I belong to you," she whispered, her voice barely audible over the wind.

And for the first time, the darkness answered.

"Yes. You do."

Chapter 15: The Boundaries of Blood

As the years passed, her siblings began to drift away, like leaves caught in a current. One by one, they slipped from the shadowed depths of the forest, their footsteps lighter and more hesitant, their voices quieting like whispers fading in the distance. They left for the edges of the forest, then beyond, where sunlight stretched across fields and houses dotted the horizon—a world that grew ever more foreign to the feral daughter.

For her siblings, stepping away from the forest was stepping into something new. They adapted quickly, adjusting to the routines and rituals of the nearby town, where each day was carefully ordered, every moment predictable. They made friends, picked up habits foreign to the feral daughter, and soon even their memories of the woods dimmed into something like a strange dream.

At first, they returned often, taking paths they'd once run wild along together. They'd try to speak to her, coaxing her to come with them, but her feral nature had taken root too deeply. Her responses were mostly gestures and guttural sounds, her language shaped by the forest more than by words. She could feel their hesitation, their quiet fear, growing each time they visited. She was no longer the sister they'd once known; she was something wild, something that moved with the same unpredictability as the creatures she shared the woods with.

Soon enough, her siblings visited less and less. Their voices, once familiar, became faint echoes in her mind, until they were only memories hanging like mist between the trees. And as they drifted farther, she felt a subtle weight settle into her chest, a strange emptiness she couldn't fully understand. Her blood had bound her to them once, but that bond was fraying, weakened by time and distance, and the pull of the forest filled the spaces they left behind.

It was in those hollow moments that the darkness began to speak again, louder and more insistent, sensing her isolation, feeding off her vulnerability. It pressed against her mind, whispering that they had abandoned her, that they had never truly understood her, that they had left her here to rot.

"They fear you," it would hiss, its voice slithering through her thoughts. "You belong to me now. They are nothing but the fleeting memories of a world that forgot you."

The darkness had a presence, a looming weight she could feel in the spaces between the trees, in the shadows that pooled underfoot like ink. It grew bolder, appearing as a faint shadow that twisted in the periphery of her vision, always just out of reach. She knew, somehow, that it had been waiting for her, watching her grow into the isolation, biding its time until she was ready to hear its call.

In her bones, she felt the presence of something ancient and restless—a creature older than the trees, a power that lay buried deep in the soil, seeping up like venom through the roots, into the veins of every creature that walked these woods. It became her only companion, a force she both feared and relied on. It was something sinister, something that filled the hollows her family had left behind.

And then one evening, as the sun dipped below the trees and the forest darkened around her, she felt a new urge rising within—a need to see her family, to touch that distant world once more. She moved through the woods toward the border, where the treeline met the edge of the town, her heart pounding with a strange, hollow ache.

She waited, watching her family's home from a distance. She could see someone through the window: her sister, older now, her face marked with lines she didn't recognize. Her father sat in a chair by the fire, his face pale and drawn, his eyes hollowed by the grief he'd carried since the day they'd lost her to the pines. They looked so different, like strangers in the light. She didn't recognize their voices anymore, their words softened and smoothed by a life that had moved on.

She longed to reach out to them, to call out, but something held her back—a fear, a dread that wrapped around her like chains. She knew, deep down, that they would never accept her, not as she was now. She was part of the forest, part of the darkness that had shaped her. They could never understand.

As she watched, a faint whisper echoed in her mind, a reminder that she would never belong in their world, not anymore. She was bound to the forest, tethered to the shadows, and the darkness was her only companion.

"They have forgotten all about you," it murmured, its voice laced with bitterness. "They have chosen their world, and you have chosen yours."

And in that moment, something broke within her. She turned away, her heart heavy with a sorrow that twisted into anger, an anger that throbbed like a wound she couldn't heal. She was a ghost to them now, a figment lost to the wilderness, and they would never understand the depth of her loneliness, her isolation.

As she walked back into the woods, the darkness enveloped her, its cold embrace a comfort in the void her family had left behind. She belonged to the forest, to the shadows that had shaped her, and she knew, with a fierce, bitter certainty, that she would never belong anywhere else. The darkness was all she had now, and she would embrace it fully, let it consume her until there was nothing left but the wild, untamed creature she had become.

The days that followed were uneasy ones for her sister and father, the only family members left at home, a blur of silent meals and nervous glances exchanged across the table. Evelyn felt it first, the strange absence that hung heavy in the air, as though a limb had been severed from their family and left an aching wound. The forest, which they had once known as home, seemed less inviting now, less forgiving. It had claimed her sister, and she knew, in the way one knows the sky will darken before a storm, that she would not be returning in any way she would recognize.

The oldest sibling, her brother, couldn't shake the memory of his last sight of her, standing on the edge of the clearing, half-hidden in shadow. There had been a wildness in her eyes, a look that was both foreign and painfully familiar, as though she were already drifting into another world—one where they couldn't follow. He had felt her slipping away for years, but now it was final, an unspoken severance that gnawed at his insides.

When he and his other siblings left the forest for the last time, it was with a sense of surrender. The rural farming community welcomed them, but the transition felt hollow, as if they were ghosts drifting between two worlds. The laughter of neighbors, the smell of bread baking, the orderly rows of fields—they should have been comforting, reminders of a life that was warm and human. But instead, every step away from the forest felt like betrayal, like they were abandoning a part of themselves they could never recover.

He remembered his mother seemed the most affected, though she tried to hide it. In the evenings, those years ago, she would sit by the window, her eyes fixed on the line of trees that marked the forest's edge, her hands clasped tightly in her lap. She rarely spoke, as if words had become meaningless in the face of what had happened, as if there was no language that could capture the loss that gnawed at her heart.

One night, as the family sat together, a chill settled over the room, a quiet, eerie feeling that made their skin prickle. The mother closed her eyes, a single tear slipping down her cheek as a whisper seemed to drift through the open window, a voice soft and mournful, laced with longing. It sounded like her daughter's voice, but it carried a strange, hollow quality, as though it were reaching across an impossible distance, across the void of something vast and ancient.

The family froze, each of them hearing the whisper but afraid to acknowledge it. They wanted to believe it was just the wind, a trick of their grief. But deep down, they knew better. The forest had taken their sister, twisted her, transformed her, and now it called to them, reminding them that she was still out there, a shadow among shadows, forever bound to the darkness that had claimed her.

In the days that followed, her siblings began to have nightmares—visions of their sister wandering the forest, her form merging with the shadows, her eyes empty and haunted. They would wake in cold sweats, the image of her lingering in their minds, a reminder that the ties between them had not been severed, not truly. The forest had taken her, yes, but it had not erased their connection; it had merely buried it beneath layers of fear and darkness.

And in those quiet, stolen moments, as they lay awake in their beds, they could almost feel her presence, as if she were standing just beyond the edge of their sight, watching, waiting. The forest was calling to them, too, whispering promises, temptations to return, to seek her out, to join her in the shadows.

But they knew, deep down, that to answer that call would be to surrender, to fall prey to the same darkness that had claimed their sister. It was a battle they fought every day, a struggle to resist the pull of the forest, to keep their lives anchored in the warmth of the world outside. And though they tried to move on, to build new lives and bury the past, the memories of her lingered, an unbreakable thread that tied them to the forest and to the darkness that had taken root in its depths.

Yet, no matter how hard they tried to forget, to ignore the whispers, they knew that the forest would always be waiting, a silent, patient guardian of their sister's soul—a soul that was no longer wholly human, no longer theirs, but something darker, something bound eternally to the wild, unyielding heart of the woods.

Even now, years later, the nightmares still came. The voice on the wind. They had abandoned their sister to the Pine Barrens. Sacrificing her for their own sanity only to be haunted by her every night.

Chapter 16: The Hollowing

The air was thick, suffocating, as if the forest itself held its breath, waiting, watching. The feral daughter sat alone in the hollow, her body wrapped in shadows as if they were a second skin. She felt the darkness around her, coiling tighter with every breath, filling every empty space within her. It was like drowning, but she welcomed it.

Somewhere, in the distance, a wolf howled. Its cry was long and mournful, a sound that carried with it a hollow ache she could feel in her chest. It struck a part of her she'd thought she'd buried, a place she had sealed away when she had given herself over to the forest, to the ancient force that claimed her.

She had felt this sadness before, on the nights when her siblings were still young, and they huddled together around a fire, their faces lit by the flickering orange light. Those nights had been warm, safe, when the world felt small and close, with no dark corners lurking just out of sight. She could remember them vaguely, the laughter, the warmth of her sister's hand, the murmur of voices against the background hum of the woods.

But they felt like memories from someone else's life. That warmth was gone now, replaced by a chill that settled deep into her bones. It was a loneliness so profound it seemed to consume her, but she wore it like armor. She had no choice; she belonged here, in the heart of the woods, where the light never quite touched the ground.

In the days following her surrender to the darkness, she had come to realize that the forest was not simply a place. It was a thing alive, an entity with its own wants, its own needs. It had been waiting for someone like her—someone who was wild enough, lost enough, empty enough to fill.

It was filling her now, taking the fragments of her old self, the scraps of her memories, and consuming them until there was nothing left but the raw, wild thing she had become. And with each piece it took, she felt herself slipping further into the void, becoming part of the ancient, twisted soul of the forest itself.

As the days passed, she found herself wandering farther into the depths, drawn to places she had once feared, to shadows that moved with a life of their own. There were whispers in the air, faint murmurs that seemed to come from nowhere and everywhere at once, voices that filled her mind with thoughts that were not her own.

They told her things—secrets about the forest, about the creatures that roamed these woods long before her family had settled here. They spoke of things that hunted in the dark, things with teeth like knives and eyes that glowed with a sickly green light. They spoke of things older than the trees, older than the land itself.

And in the quietest moments, when the wind died down and the only sound was her own heartbeat, they told her of her family. They showed her flashes of her siblings, now older, faces lined with worry and exhaustion, haunted by memories they could not escape. She saw her mother, her face pale and drawn, her eyes rimmed with red as she sat at the edge of the forest, waiting, hoping for a child who would never return.

The sight twisted something deep within her, an ache she couldn't name, a pain that felt like it was tearing her apart from the inside. She had wanted to go back, once. She had thought of leaving the forest, of stepping back into the world she had known. But that was before. Before the darkness had claimed her, before she had seen the truth.

Her family had moved on. They had left her here, buried her in their minds like some tragic story they could forget. To them, she was a ghost, a shadow lost to the woods. And maybe that was all she had ever been—a ghost waiting to fade.

"Do you miss them?" the darkness whispered, its voice curling around her mind like smoke.

She closed her eyes, her breath hitching as the words sank in. She did miss them, in a way that hurt more than she could bear. She missed the way they had laughed, the way they had looked at her with love instead of fear. She missed the warmth of human touch, the feeling of belonging somewhere, of being someone.

But those things belonged to a past she could never reclaim. They were lost to her now, just as she was lost to them.

"They never truly cared for you," the darkness continued, its tone soft, coaxing. "They left you here, abandoned you. They never loved you."

She let the words sink in, feeling the weight of them settle in her chest. It was true. They had left her. They had chosen to walk away, to build new lives, to forget about the sister who had stayed behind. They had moved on, and she had been left to the shadows, to the silence of the forest.

And yet, as much as she wanted to believe the darkness, as much as she longed to surrender to the bitterness that threatened to consume her, there was a part of her—a small, fragile part—that still remembered what it felt like to love them. To be loved by them. It was a piece of herself she had tried to bury, but it clung to her like a ghost, refusing to let go.

In the dead of night, when the forest was silent and the shadows seemed to press in around her, she could feel it—the faint echo of her family's love, a memory she couldn't quite erase. It was a weakness, a fracture in the armor she had built around herself. And the darkness knew it.

"They will forget you," it whispered, its voice cold and certain. "They will live their lives, and you will be nothing more than a story they tell on dark nights. You will be a memory, nothing more."

The words cut through her like a knife, sharp and unforgiving. She clenched her fists, her nails digging into her palms as she fought to hold back the tears that threatened to spill. She wanted to let go, to give herself fully to the darkness, to erase every trace of the girl she had once been.

But as she sat there, alone in the heart of the forest, she realized that she couldn't. There was still a part of her that remembered, a part of her that refused to fade.

And so she remained, caught between two worlds—the wild, untamed darkness that had claimed her, and the faint, fragile memory of a family she could never return to. It was a cruel, endless limbo, a hollowing that left her empty and aching, a creature caught between love and despair.

The darkness sensed her hesitation, and it tightened its grip, pressing down on her with a weight that left her breathless. It whispered promises of power, of freedom, of a life without pain or fear. All she had to do was let go. All she had to do was surrender.

But as the night stretched on, and the first light of dawn crept over the trees, she knew that she couldn't. She was bound to the forest, to the darkness, but she was also bound to the memory of her family, to the faint, flickering hope that one day, somehow, they would remember her.

And so she waited, trapped in a world of shadows and silence, a creature torn between the savage bond of the forest and the fragile echo of her humanity.

Chapter 17: Into the Heart of Darkness

In the following days, the forest grew denser, as if alive and pressing closer around her, twisting in on itself like a labyrinth of branches and shadows. The air felt heavier, saturated with a kind of malevolent quiet. Even the creatures she had once felt kinship with—the wolves, the ravens, the deer—had grown silent in her presence. They sensed the change in her, the darkness that clung to her skin like a second shadow. It was as if the forest itself had conspired to forge her into something wholly its own, a keeper of its secrets, an unwilling child of its hunger.

The darkness grew more intense, more possessive, its whispers morphing from soft murmurs to feverish demands that echoed through her mind. She could hear it even in the quiet moments, its voice low and insistent, like a pulse just beneath the surface of her consciousness. It promised her power, a kind of twisted strength that came from forsaking all that had once been human within her. And in return, all it asked was her loyalty, her obedience, her soul.

"You are not one of them, you are one of us," it would say, the words curling around her like tendrils of smoke. "They left you behind. They cast you out. You belong here, with me, where you will never be alone again."

The girl could feel its pull growing stronger, a magnetic force drawing her ever deeper into the darkest reaches of the forest. Her steps became aimless, driven by an instinct to search for something she couldn't name but could feel in her bones. Her once wild and fierce independence was now shackled to this relentless compulsion, a need that clawed at her insides. She was no longer the master of her own will; she was something possessed, tethered to a power that would not release her.

The whispers guided her to the center of the forest, to a place she had never dared to go, where the trees were ancient and gnarled, their trunks twisted into grotesque shapes that seemed almost human. The ground was covered in a thick layer of moss that muffled her footsteps, and the air was cold, colder than it had ever been, as if this part of the woods had never felt the warmth of the sun.

Here, the darkness took form. A figure began to emerge from the shadows, its outline indistinct, more of an absence of light than a presence. It had no face, no clear shape, but its essence was overpowering, a primal force that reeked of decay and malice. She could feel its eyes on her, though she could see none, and in that gaze, she felt stripped bare, her soul exposed and vulnerable.

"You belong to me," it said, the words slithering into her mind like a toxin. "You always have, and you always will."

She fell to her knees, her hands pressing into the cold, damp earth, her heart pounding with a strange, desperate longing she couldn't understand. She wanted to run, to escape, but there was nowhere to go. The forest was all around her, enclosing her in a cage of roots and shadows, and the darkness was at its core, watching her with a terrible hunger.

A memory surfaced then, of her mother's face, the warmth in her eyes, the gentle touch of her hand. It was a memory she hadn't allowed herself to think of in years, a sliver of the life she had left behind. But now it felt distant, as if it belonged to someone else. She couldn't remember the sound of her mother's voice or the exact shape of her smile; those details had faded, replaced by the cold, empty presence of the darkness that had claimed her.

But that memory, faint as it was, stirred something within her—a spark of defiance, a reminder that she had once been more than this, more than the creature she had become. She forced herself to stand, her legs shaking, her hands clenched into fists. She looked into the void where the darkness waited, she felt a glimmer of resistance.

"I don't belong to you," she whispered, her voice barely audible, but filled with a quiet strength that surprised her.

The darkness recoiled, a hiss echoing through the trees, but it quickly regained its composure, its presence swelling around her like a wave, pressing down on her with a force that stole her breath. It laughed, a sound that was neither human nor animal, a twisted, mocking echo that reverberated through her skull.

"You think you can escape me?" it sneered. "You think they will take you back? You are tainted, marked by the forest. You are mine, little creature, and there is no place for you out there. You would be nothing without me."

The words cut deep, striking at the heart of her fear, her loneliness. It was right— she was no longer the girl her family had known. She had become something else, something wild and untamed, shaped by the shadows and the silence of the forest. But even so, there was a part of her that refused to yield, a part of her that remembered the light, the warmth, the love she had once felt.

With a surge of determination, she took a step back, breaking the spell of the darkness that had held her captive for so long. She turned and ran, her feet pounding against the forest floor, her breath coming in ragged gasps. She didn't know where she was going, only that she had to get away, to escape the suffocating presence that pursued her.

The darkness roared, its rage filling the air with a sound that made the trees shudder and the ground tremble. It lashed out, sending tendrils of shadow snaking after her, but she was faster, her instincts sharp and unrelenting. She dodged and weaved through the trees, her body moving with a grace that was almost animalistic, driven by a primal urge to survive.

But as she ran, she felt the weight of the darkness pressing down on her, felt its fury searing into her mind. It would not let her go, not without a fight. And she knew, in the depths of her soul, that this was only the beginning—that the darkness would haunt her, hunt her, until it reclaimed what it believed was its own.

Yet, for the first time, in such a long time, she felt hope—a small, fragile thing, but enough to keep her moving, enough to remind her that she was still alive, still free, still fighting.

As she vanished into the trees, the darkness watched, its shape dissolving into the shadows, but its voice lingered, a whisper that echoed through the forest, promising vengeance.

"You can run, little creature," it murmured, "but you will never be free."

Chapter 18: Whispers on the Wind

Rumors of a strange presence in the woods began to drift through the nearby village, whispered between townsfolk over fences and cups of coffee. People spoke of sightings, of a shadowy figure that lingered just out of sight, watching with eyes that gleamed in the night. Children dared each other to enter the edge of the forest at dusk, only to flee at the crack of a branch or the rustle of leaves, their imaginations fed by the stories that grew wilder with each retelling.

It wasn't long before the stories found their way back to her family. Her fathers face grew pale as neighbors recounted the tales—of animal tracks that seemed almost human, of strange noises that carried through the night, and of the unsettling feeling that something, someone, was watching from the woods. Her siblings, who had tried to settle into village life, felt the hairs rise on the backs of their necks each time they heard the stories, each one reminding them of what they had left behind. They knew, deep down, that the forest was keeping their sister in its hold, changing her into something they could no longer recognize.

Late one night, her sister awoke from a restless sleep, drawn by an unshakable urge to look outside. She wrapped a shawl around her shoulders, stepping to the window that faced the forest. The moonlight spilled across the ground, illuminating the edge of the trees, where, for a fleeting moment, she thought she saw a shadow—a figure half-hidden in darkness. Her heart skipped a beat. It looked like her feral sister, standing there, watching, yet there was something unearthly about her, something that made her sister's skin prickle with dread.

But just as quickly as she'd seen it, the figure vanished into the trees, leaving only the memory of that haunting presence. Evelyn stayed by the window, her hand pressed to the glass, feeling a hollow ache in her chest. It was as if her sister were calling out to her, from the depths of the woods, reaching across the boundary that separated them. Yet she knew, with an almost painful clarity, that the sister she had known was gone, replaced by something darker, something that no longer belonged to the world of light and warmth.

As dawn broke, Evelyn finally stepped away from the window, her face drawn and weary. She hadn't slept a wink, but she knew she could no longer ignore the pull of the forest, the silent summons that had haunted her dreams. She went into town and gathered her siblings, her voice shaking as she told them what she'd seen, what she felt. Her oldest brother listened in silence, his expression unreadable, but in his eyes, she saw the same flicker of dread she felt in her heart.

The family made a decision that morning—a promise to each other. They would not return to the forest, not even for her. To go back was to risk being claimed by the same darkness that had taken their sister. It was a painful choice, but they knew it was the only way to keep themselves safe from the force that had twisted her, that had woven itself into her very being.

And in the forest, she felt their decision. She felt the severing of the last thin strand that had connected her to the world beyond the trees. It was a sharp, aching pain, but it was fleeting, quickly swallowed by the whispers that enveloped her, by the cold, familiar presence that had become her only companion. She belonged to the woods now, bound by a force older and darker than she could comprehend.

As the sun rose higher, her form melted back into the shadows, her figure merging with the trees, her eyes gleaming in the half-light. She was neither human nor beast, but something in between, something that existed in the spaces where light couldn't reach. And with each passing day, she let go of the girl she had once been, surrendering fully to the voice that guided her, the sinister force that pulsed through the forest.

To the villagers, she became a myth, a ghostly legend spoken of in hushed voices. But to her family, she was a painful memory, a reminder of the darkness that lurked beyond the edge of their lives. And for her, they became little more than fading dreams, echoes of a life that no longer held any meaning.

She belonged to the forest now. And the forest, with all its ancient shadows and whispered secrets, belonged to her.

The forest was alive in ways the villagers would never understand. Beneath its tangled roots, in the spaces between the trees, there was a pulse—an ancient rhythm that whispered secrets only she could hear. As she drifted deeper into the woods, the forest began to change her. She could feel it taking root inside her, each step grounding her further in its secrets, each breath filling her lungs with something darker, thicker, a sensation that clung to her soul. She became attuned to every rustling leaf, every crack of a twig, every murmur in the canopy above.

The once-familiar sounds of animals scurrying or owls calling at night now seemed to carry messages, coded in the forest's own language. The wind through the branches was no longer just the wind; it was a voice, low and coaxing, like a song she was beginning to remember. She no longer feared the darkness that clung to the forest's depths. Instead, she felt herself becoming one with it, as though the darkness were a lover drawing her close, wrapping her in its cold embrace.

As days passed, her memories of her family began to blur, slipping into dreamlike fragments. Their voices became echoes, distant and hollow, easily swallowed by the trees. She could hardly remember their faces now, only flashes of pale skin and eyes that once held warmth—a warmth she had no use for anymore. It was as if the forest were replacing them in her mind, filling the void with images of shadows and things that lurked in the spaces humans dared not tread.

The voice that had once terrified her now felt like a part of her. It was no longer something she feared; it was a companion, a constant, darkly comforting presence that guided her through the night. When it whispered to her, she could feel her mind bend and sway, as if her thoughts were threads the voice could pull and twist. It filled her with visions—sometimes of things that had happened long ago, dark moments hidden in the forest's depths; other times, it showed her glimpses of what might be, twisted images of her own future.

The visions grew more intense with each day, scenes of strange rituals and shadowy figures dancing beneath moonlight. She saw herself among them, her skin painted with earth, her eyes feral, lips drawn back in a snarl as she became something not quite human, something older and wilder. The voice urged her on, told her these were her people now, her kin of shadow and bone, the ones who would never abandon her.

She began to forget the boundaries of her own mind, her thoughts blending with the whispers, her sense of self dissolving into something more primitive, more animalistic. Hunger felt different now, not just for food, but for the thrill of the hunt, the rush of stalking something unaware. She would slip through the trees with a predator's grace, her senses sharpened, her body moving as if guided by some instinct deep within her.

On one of these nights, she came across a deer, grazing quietly in a small clearing. Her breath stilled, her pulse slowed, and she crouched, waiting. The voice urged her forward, filling her with a savage exhilaration, a dark joy that pulsed through her veins as she crept closer. She could feel the power within her, a force that had been there all along but was now unbound, let loose by the forest's dark call.

The deer's head lifted suddenly, ears twitching as it sensed her presence. But it was too late. She lunged, a flash of movement through the underbrush, feeling the thrill of the chase as it bolted away. She didn't catch it, but the chase itself was intoxicating. She realized then that it wasn't the kill she wanted; it was the feeling of wild abandon, the primal thrill that filled her chest as she gave herself over to the hunt.

The more time she spent in the forest, the less she felt tethered to anything outside it. She no longer needed the constraints of language or the rules of her old world. She understood now that she was part of something ancient, something far beyond the simplicity of human life. The trees became her companions, their branches stretching toward her like the arms of friends, offering her solace. The darkness beneath their boughs held her close, cradling her in shadows that felt like home.

One night, as she wandered through the forest, the voice grew louder, more insistent, filling her mind with images that twisted and blurred, forcing her to confront the truth of what she was becoming. She saw herself through the forest's eyes—a creature of shadows, her skin pale and glistening like damp stone, her hair tangled with leaves, her eyes wild and feral, reflecting the cold light of the moon. She was no longer the girl who had wandered in; she was something other, something primal.

"You belong to me," the voice whispered, its words sinking into her bones, a dark promise she could feel wrapping around her. "And you always will."

She felt the final pieces of her humanity slipping away, like petals falling from a dying flower, leaving only the raw essence of who she was: a child of the forest, born anew in its shadows, bound to it in ways that no human could understand. And as she stood there, staring up at the sky through the skeletal fingers of the trees, she felt a fierce, wild joy welling within her, a savage acceptance of the darkness she had become.

The forest was no longer just her home; it was her master, her guide, her only kin. She belonged to it now, and it belonged to her.

Chapter 19: The Thirteenth Child

The days in the forest became a haze of shadows and silence, each one blending seamlessly into the next. She felt a growing sense of purpose, an underlying hum that thrummed through her bones, but she couldn't name it. She only knew that something was guiding her steps, like a current pulling her deeper and deeper, beyond the places she had known, into the parts of the woods where the sunlight barely reached, and the air felt thick with secrets.

One evening, as she wandered further than ever before, she came across an old clearing. In the center lay stones, rough and ancient, arranged in a circle that seemed older than time itself. Her eyes lingered on each stone, and something inside her shifted, a prickling sense that she had seen this place before, though she couldn't recall when or how.

As she approached the stones, she began to hear whispers—not the familiar murmur of the forest, but voices, ancient and fractured, like memories etched into the air. They spoke of a child, one who would emerge from darkness, bound to the forest, the thirteenth child born to a mother who had lost so many others. Her heart hammered in her chest, each beat bringing forth images of her mother's sorrow, memories of her distant siblings, and visions of small graves hidden in shadows.

It was then that she realized the truth—she was the thirteenth child.

The stories she had overheard as a young girl came rushing back. In whispers, the villagers would tell tales of a child born from sorrow, a child who would carry the weight of death upon their shoulders. Her mother had borne twelve children before her, many of whom never took a breath, leaving a shadow of grief over the family. But the thirteenth child was different; the thirteenth child would be marked by the forest, would belong to it in ways that no one could understand.

The legend, as the whispers told it, spoke of this thirteenth child—the last child, a soul bound to the woods, who would hold a darkness within them so deep that even death could not claim it. She was a child born to bridge the world of the living and the dead, to become one with the forest and guard its secrets.

Her mind reeled as the pieces began to fall into place. She wasn't simply a lost girl, abandoned to the wilds. She was part of something greater, something ancient. The forest hadn't taken her by chance; it had claimed her, knowing that she was the fulfillment of an old prophecy, one that had waited for generations.

As she knelt among the stones, memories came unbidden, pieces of her mother's face, her sad eyes, the worn lines etched into her brow. Her mother had never spoken of her lost children, had kept that sorrow buried deep. But now, in the forest's embrace, she understood it. She was meant to carry the weight of those lost souls, to be their voice, their connection to the world they had left behind.

The whispers grew louder, speaking to her directly now, filling her with visions of what was to come. She saw herself as the forest's sentinel, a shadow that roamed its depths, both protector and warden. The dark force that had woven itself into her life was not simply a monster in the woods; it was a part of her, a force that had waited for her birth to rise, to find its vessel.

"You are the child born of darkness," the voices whispered, echoing through her mind like a drumbeat. "The thirteenth child, the one who will hold the forest's secrets and guard its soul."

The realization sent a shiver down her spine, but it was quickly replaced by something else—a fierce pride, a sense of purpose that filled the hollow spaces inside her. She belonged to the forest, not as a victim, but as its chosen guardian, its last line of defense. She was more than the feral girl she had thought herself to be; she was the embodiment of an ancient promise, a being that transcended humanity.

As the truth settled within her, the shadows seemed to shift, embracing her fully, welcoming her into their depths. The dark force that had haunted her became something familiar, something that pulsed within her own blood. It was no longer a separate entity; it was a part of her, a twin flame that flickered alongside her own spirit.

She rose from the stones, feeling the weight of her new identity settling on her shoulders like a mantle. She was the thirteenth child, the one born to fulfill the prophecy, to carry the weight of the forest's secrets and protect its borders. And with each step she took, she felt herself transform, becoming less a girl and more a legend, a being woven from shadow and bone, destined to haunt the forest forever.

In the village, her family felt a chill ripple through their hearts, an unspoken dread that told them their sister was gone—not lost, but transformed, something both beautiful and terrifying, something that belonged to the woods in ways they would never understand.

As she emerged from the clearing and wove her way back through the trees, her steps felt both familiar and foreign, as though she were walking with someone else's feet. Her limbs moved with a fluidity that hadn't been there before, a grace that was almost animalistic. Her fingers flexed at her sides, sharper somehow, and as she caught sight of her reflection in a shallow pool, she paused, staring into her own eyes.

They had changed. The familiar amber had deepened into something darker, flecked with shadows that swirled and shifted, almost as if the forest had taken root within her gaze. Her pupils, wide and black, seemed to draw in the light, absorbing it like an endless void. It was a small change, but undeniable, and when she reached up to touch her face, her fingers brushed against the faint, almost invisible lines of something new—small, subtle marks along her skin, like cracks in porcelain, as if the forest were carving itself into her.

Her hair, once wild and tangled, had taken on a darker, more lustrous sheen, blending seamlessly with the shadows around her, as if it were more a part of the forest than of her. She felt stronger, faster, her movements as silent as the whispers that followed her. Even her scent was changing—no longer that of a young girl who lived in the woods but something earthier, deeper, tinged with decay and damp moss, like the forest floor after a storm.

The change was more than skin deep. Her demeanor, once wild but gentle, was shifting. She no longer felt the urge to flee from the darkness; instead, she craved it. Her mind, which had once been a blend of human thought and animal instinct, was being twisted, shaped by something else entirely. She began to feel a quiet hunger that had nothing to do with food, a need to possess, to hunt, to dominate. The forest was no longer a home; it was her kingdom, her domain, and anything that entered it would do so under her watchful, predatory eye.

And with this transformation came a sense of isolation, a profound separation from her family, even the siblings who had once wandered the woods with her. She felt no longing for them, only a cold recognition that they would never understand what she had become. They had escaped, leaving her to her fate, while she had embraced it, accepted it, and let it seep into her very bones. A faint bitterness curled in her chest, not quite anger, but something close—a resentment that fueled her dark thoughts, strengthening her bond with the shadows that danced around her.

In time, even her movements changed. She no longer walked as a human; she glided, her steps almost soundless, her posture low and predatory. She could feel the shadows guiding her, each step aligned with an unspoken rhythm, a heartbeat that pulsed from the forest floor itself. The darkness became a cloak, wrapping her in its embrace, making her invisible even in the dimmest light.

But the forest was not done with her. She felt it constantly, its silent promises, its whispered words, coaxing her to relinquish the last vestiges of her humanity, to become something entirely new, entirely of its making. And with each day, each moonlit night spent prowling through the underbrush, she felt herself slipping further, leaving behind the girl she had been, becoming a creature of shadows and ancient earth.

And as she moved through the woods, she realized something strange yet undeniable: she no longer remembered her own name. It was as if the forest had stripped her identity from her, replacing it with something nameless, something eternal. She was no longer a girl, no longer a daughter. She was simply the Thirteenth Child, the forest's own—a haunting presence, a specter bound to the trees and stones, more ghost than human, more shadow than flesh.

Chapter 20: Bound to the Shadows

The days passed in a blur of endless twilight, each moment pulling her deeper into the heart of the forest. Her human memories had faded, replaced by instinct and ritual, a silent communion with the woods around her. She no longer felt like an outsider peering into the mysteries of the forest; she was part of them, woven into the very fabric of the undergrowth and shadows. But with each passing day, a strange compulsion grew—a quiet, persistent pull to seek out her family, to show them what she had become.

The thought lingered like a thorn in her mind, a mix of resentment and something that bordered on yearning. She wanted them to see her, to understand the sacrifice that had been demanded of her. She was no longer their sister, their daughter; she was something far older and more powerful. She imagined stepping out of the shadows, watching the horror dawn on their faces as they looked upon her now, seeing not the girl they had left behind, but a creature touched by darkness.

The forest seemed to respond to her desire. That evening, the shadows grew heavier, curling around her in tendrils, leading her along paths she hadn't walked since she was young. She moved with purpose, her steps as quiet as a whisper, her breath slow and shallow, as if the air itself feared to disturb the silence. The trees arched above her like guardians, bending to shield her as she approached the edge of the woods.

She caught sight of her family's cabin in the dim light, a pale shape in the distance, almost ghostly in its familiarity. From her place hidden among the trees, she watched as her sister moved outside, her steps weary, her shoulders hunched as if under a great weight. Her father stood nearby, scanning the trees, his eyes filled with a haunted, restless look, as though he sensed the presence of something terrible just beyond the tree line.

For a moment, the 13th child felt a flicker of something—an old, buried emotion, something close to longing. But it vanished as quickly as it came, replaced by an almost cruel satisfaction. They looked broken, burdened by the same dread that had once followed her steps through the forest. She wanted them to see her, but not as daughter or sister. She wanted them to witness the creature they had abandoned to the shadows.

As she stepped forward, a low whisper echoed through her mind—the forest's voice, ancient and inescapable.

"Show them. Show them what they have lost."

She obeyed, emerging from the shadows, her form almost unrecognizable. Her skin, pale and luminous in the moonlight, seemed etched with faint lines that glowed like cracks in stone. Her eyes were black pools, reflecting none of the warmth they once held, only the endless depth of the forest. She no longer wore rags or remnants of her old life; the forest had clothed her in layers of leaves and vines, twisted into a dress that moved with her, shifting as if it were alive.

Her family froze, their faces a mask of terror and disbelief. Her sisters hand rose to her mouth, a choked sob escaping her lips, while her father took a step back, his eyes widening as if he couldn't fully comprehend what he was seeing.

"Is it... is it really you?" her sisters voice was barely a whisper, trembling with a fragile hope.

But the 13th child said nothing. She simply stared, her gaze cold and hollow, letting them feel the weight of the void between them. She wanted them to see that she no longer belonged to them, that she was something they could never again reclaim.

Yet, as her sister stepped closer, her trembling hand reaching out, the 13th child felt the forest's hold tighten around her, binding her, reminding her of the promise she had made.

"You are mine," the dark voice whispered, louder this time, filling her mind, blotting out the faint thread of human memory that flickered within her. "And you will remain."

She turned away, retreating into the shadows without a backward glance, leaving her family standing alone in the moonlight, their cries following her as she disappeared. It was a cruel mercy, one she offered without hesitation.

As she melted into the darkness, she felt herself merge more fully with the forest, her human heart fading, replaced by something colder, more resilient. She was no longer bound by family or love. She belonged only to the woods, a child of prophecy and shadow, a sentinel that would guard its secrets for eternity.

And in the silent, endless night, the 13th child found her true home at long last.

Chapter 21: Blood for the Black Tree

Under the canopy of twisted branches and the ever-present fog that wrapped itself around her like a shroud, she felt her purpose crystallize. The black tree loomed in her mind—a towering figure of gnarled bark and deadened roots, its hollow core breathing with an ancient, insidious life that demanded blood. She could feel it deep within her, like a hunger gnawing at her very soul, a force that now commanded her every thought and action.

It began subtly at first, a low whisper in the back of her mind. But the voice of the forest grew louder, pulsing, vibrating with a singular command that echoed through her veins: "Feed me. Revive me."

The first sacrifice came easily. She encountered a lone hiker near the boundary of the woods, his mind distracted, unaware of the creature watching him from the shadows. She moved with the precision of a predator, silent and swift. Before he could even register her presence, it was over. His blood soaked into the forest floor, and she felt the earth pulse beneath her as the forest drank deeply, its roots spreading out like veins, drawing life back into the black tree.

With each sacrifice, the forest's hold on her grew stronger. The black tree's bark began to shift, taking on a darker, glossier hue, as if the blood she offered it was seeping into its core, reviving it inch by inch. The air grew colder, and she felt the very ground shudder as if awakening. She was no longer merely the girl from the woods; she had become an agent of the forest's wrath, a hand that brought death to fuel the tree's resurrection. The 13th Child.

But the forest wanted more.

The darkness within her festered, spreading like rot, twisting her mind until she barely recognized herself. She found herself drawn to the edges of the woods, watching the nearby town in the dead of night, her thoughts a maelstrom of violence and hunger. She moved through the shadows, picking her prey with care—stray travelers, wanderers, those whose lives would not be missed.

As she dragged their bodies through the forest, she could feel the tree's pull growing stronger. She left each one beneath its towering limbs, their blood seeping into the ground, their life force feeding the ancient roots. She watched as the black tree's bark grew denser, its branches stretching, clawing toward the sky, bearing strange, twisted leaves that whispered in a language older than time.

Each sacrifice brought her closer to the black tree, binding her spirit to it until she could no longer tell where she ended and it began. The twisted voices of the forest filled her mind, their chorus of whispers growing louder with each passing day, pressing her forward in an unending cycle of blood and ritual. She felt nothing as she carried out the killings, only the satisfaction of fulfilling her duty, of feeding the hunger that pulsed in her veins.

One night, as she knelt beneath the black tree after her latest offering, she felt it—an ancient, dark power swirling within the roots, coiling up through the branches. It reached out to her, wrapping her in a cold embrace, filling her mind with images of the forest's past, of forgotten rituals and sacrifices made in its name. She saw the faces of those who had come before her, guardians and devotees of the forest, all succumbing to the tree's insatiable hunger, just as she had.

And then, the tree spoke.

"You are mine now, bound by blood and darkness. You shall keep this forest alive, keep the world away, for as long as you breathe."

She felt her body surrender to the command, every fiber of her being bending to the will of the black tree. She no longer fought it, no longer remembered what it felt like to resist. She belonged to the forest, an eternal servant, an instrument of its vengeance and hunger.

As she rose, her hands stained with blood, her mind filled with a savage purpose. She would continue to feed the forest, to bring life to its roots, to see the black tree rise again in all its terrible glory. She was no longer human, no longer bound by mortal constraints. She was the forest's dark heart, a specter bound to its shadows, an unyielding force of nature.

And as she disappeared into the darkness, her steps silent as death, the forest stirred, ready to claim whatever life dared enter its domain, its thirst for blood awakened and eternal.

The black tree stood taller now, its towering branches twisting together in grotesque patterns, reaching skyward like skeletal arms clawing at the heavens. Dark sap oozed from the bark, thick as blood, dripping onto the ground and creating a circle of lifeless soil around its base. The roots stretched farther than they ever had, writhing through the earth like veins, hungry and insatiable, drinking up the life she brought, growing stronger with every sacrifice.

She stood before it, feeling a surge of power radiate through her, linking her spirit to the tree's malevolence. Her mind twisted further, consumed by a darkness that felt ancient and boundless, a force older than any human memory. She was no longer merely a vessel; she had become one with the forest's shadowed heart, an embodiment of its darkest will.

The sky above darkened, clouds swirling and gathering as if drawn to the tree's malice. A thunderous crack split the air, a sound that reverberated through the woods, sending flocks of birds scattering in a frenzy of caws and shrieks. The wind picked up, whipping through the trees, carrying a thick, suffocating mist that seemed to radiate from the black tree itself.

As she knelt, the voice returned, deep and resonant, vibrating through the roots and filling the air with its dark, all-consuming presence.

"Your offerings have brought me back, child. Now, the forest shall reclaim its domain, and those who trespass shall know the wrath of the ancient woods."

The ground trembled beneath her as the black tree's roots began to twist and coil, pushing up through the earth like massive serpents. They slithered outward, seeking to spread their darkness beyond the boundaries of the forest. Her body vibrated with the tree's power, feeling its pulse through her own veins, as if it had poured its essence into her. She was no longer a mere child of the forest; she was a guardian of its rage, a living weapon bound to its vengeance.

The roots found the bodies she had brought nearby, twisting around them, pulling them closer to the tree's base. To her horror—and delight—the corpses began to twitch and convulse, their limbs jerking as the roots animated them, binding them to the black tree's will. They rose, their eyes hollow and lifeless, yet somehow glinting with a dark obedience.

They were her army now—soulless, silent, and bound to the tree's sinister purpose.

The transformation of the black tree was almost complete. Its branches thickened, forming a canopy so dense it blotted out the light, casting the entire forest into perpetual twilight. Strange, twisted fruits began to grow from its branches, dark and pulsating with an eerie glow, each one containing the corrupted essence of the sacrifices she had offered. The tree was feeding, absorbing the life it had taken, growing ever stronger, its roots spreading far and wide, seeking to consume and corrupt all they touched.

The air grew thick with a toxic, sweet smell, a scent that could lure any living creature closer, tempting them to step into the tree's domain, where they, too, would be devoured, their essence feeding the ancient malevolence. She watched, enthralled, as the black tree continued to transform, watching as the creatures of the forest—deer, wolves, birds—were drawn toward it, as if hypnotized by the foul allure.

They gathered around its base, eyes glazed, bodies trembling. The tree's roots reached out, wrapping around each creature, pulling them into the ground, their muffled cries lost beneath the dirt as they were absorbed into the roots. The black tree glowed with an unnatural life, each sacrifice fueling its growth, its power expanding far beyond the forest.

A storm of shadows danced around her, swirling in the mist, and she understood that the forest would never be the same. It had become a realm of its own, an extension of the black tree's malignant spirit. A darkness that would stretch, slowly but surely, beyond the woods, reaching out to taint the world beyond.

She looked upon the tree, feeling its twisted life course through her, binding her to its darkness forever. She was no longer just a servant of the forest's ancient will; she was its very embodiment, a creature bound by blood and shadow, forever loyal to the black tree.

"The world will know our hunger," she whispered, her voice as hollow as the roots, as dark as the tree's soul. And as the tree's roots slithered farther into the ground, reaching toward the unsuspecting towns, she knew her dark purpose had only just begun.

Chapter 22: Shadows Beyond the Forest

The black tree had completed its transformation. It loomed with a sinister presence, its dark canopy casting the entire forest into an unnatural, suffocating darkness. The only light came from the twisted fruits that glowed faintly on its branches, casting an eerie, pulsing reddish glow across the twisted landscape.

Her transformation, too, was complete. She moved silently through the forest, her senses heightened, her eyes gleaming with a ferocious, otherworldly light. Her once-soft features had hardened, sharpened—her skin paler, her nails more like claws. Her gaze was no longer human; it carried the weight of the darkness that had claimed her, a void that seemed to suck in all light. Every step she took left a trace of decay in its wake as if the earth itself recoiled from her presence.

But it wasn't enough. The tree was alive, powerful, but it craved more—an insatiable hunger that echoed in her own mind, a gnawing void that demanded she keep feeding it.

As night fell, the darkness grew thicker, pressing against the trees, seeping into the air. The animals that had once been a part of her world no longer approached her, instead retreating into the farthest reaches of the forest. Even the wind dared not disturb the silence. It was as if the entire forest held its breath, waiting.

She wandered to the edges of the woods, where the glow of distant town lights flickered like stars on the horizon. Her siblings were there, somewhere among the humans, living ordinary lives, untouched by the darkness that had consumed her. The thought stirred something cold and bitter within her—a resentment, a fury that burned like acid.

She had tried to return to them once, to bridge the impossible distance that separated them. But now, standing under the black tree's monstrous branches, she felt only scorn for their world. They had left her behind, abandoned her to the forest. And now, they would pay.

The tree's roots stirred, sensing her dark intentions. They extended toward her, coiling around her ankles, then receded as if beckoning her to follow. She understood its command, her purpose clear.

The forest would not stay contained for much longer.

She moved through the trees, her body a shadow among shadows, blending into the darkness. Her thoughts were no longer her own but woven with the forest's hunger, its deep-rooted desire to consume. She crossed the edge of the woods, her bare feet stepping onto the dirt road that led toward town. Each step was silent, her movements as smooth and fluid as a predator stalking its prey.

As she reached the first farmhouse on the outskirts, a low, unnatural fog began to spread across the ground, seeping from the woods, slithering between the trees and over the fields, obscuring the night with a thick, stifling haze. The tree's influence had expanded, its roots pushing beneath the earth, claiming more and more of the land.

Inside the farmhouse, lights flickered, and the family inside grew uneasy. Shadows danced across the walls, shifting and writhing as if alive, and the air grew cold, carrying a strange, sweet rot that clung to the back of their throats. The father, sensing something wrong, peered out the window, his eyes straining against the darkness.

For a moment, he saw her—a pale figure standing at the edge of his field, barely visible in the thick fog. Her eyes glowed with an unnatural light, piercing the night. He felt a chill run through him, something primal, a sense that he was looking at something not of this world.

Then, she smiled—a slow, unsettling smile that bared her sharpened teeth, a flash of something inhuman, twisted and malevolent. Before he could cry out, the shadows around him closed in, filling his vision with darkness, his scream swallowed by the mist as the black tree claimed another life.

The next morning, the town awoke to a strange silence. Birds were absent, and a lingering fog shrouded the streets, casting an unshakable gloom over the town. People whispered of strange figures seen at the edges of the fields, of lights flickering and shadows moving when they shouldn't.

But none dared venture into the forest. They knew, deep in their bones, that the forest was no longer theirs to explore. It belonged to something older, something darker. And as they looked toward the trees, at the unnatural mist that clung to its edges, they couldn't shake the feeling that something was watching, waiting just beyond the shadows.

She returned to the black tree at dawn, her skin soaked in blood, her eyes burning with a satisfaction that was not her own. The tree pulsed with life, its roots reaching deeper into the earth, spreading farther. It would continue until there was nothing left untouched by its darkness.

She knelt before it, offering her loyalty in silence. And in that silence, she heard it—a low, guttural whisper, a promise and a command woven together.

"Go forth, my child. Bring them all to me."

As she rose, the forest around her stirred, a thousand dark eyes watching from the shadows, creatures drawn by the tree's call, bound to it as she was. She felt her humanity slip further away, replaced by something savage, something ancient, a darkness that would not rest until all who lived beyond the forest knew its wrath.

And as she moved, the fog spread, the shadows deepened, and the town—her family—waited, unaware of the nightmare that had already begun to seep into their lives, an unstoppable force that no mortal heart could hope to survive.

The town remained under the eerie veil of silence, the mist wrapping around buildings and creeping through alleyways like fingers reaching into every dark corner. The shadows were thicker now, heavy with an unnatural weight. Townsfolk huddled inside their homes, whispering about the strange fog that lingered, defying the morning light, refusing to dissipate. A few brave souls ventured out, feeling an odd compulsion to look toward the woods, as if something out there were calling them.

One by one, they began to disappeared into the mist.

She watched from the tree line, her eyes gleaming with a malevolent satisfaction. She was no longer just a girl of the forest—she was its hand, its will given form, her veins pulsing with the same darkness that fueled the ancient roots of the black tree. Each step she took closer to town seemed to drain color from the world, casting a dull pallor over everything in her path. The closer she drew, the more powerful she felt, as if the town itself fed her with its fear.

In the distance, she could see the farmhouse where her older siblings had taken refuge, far from the life they'd left behind in the woods. She could almost feel their dread from here, like an invisible thread binding them to her still, no matter how far they'd tried to run. She remembered them as children, their laughter, their whispers of fear when they'd felt eyes watching them from the dark. Now, she felt nothing but the pull of the tree, urging her to draw them back into its shadow.

With each step toward the farmhouse, her form seemed to shift, her limbs elongating, her nails sharp and curved. Her skin took on a deathly pallor, veins darkening beneath it. Her hair, once wild and tangled, now seemed like strands of shadow, blending into the mist that clung to her.

In her mind, voices whispered—the spirits of those long claimed by the forest, the remnants of souls who had once wandered too deep. They whispered warnings, sang twisted lullabies, all weaving into her thoughts, binding her tighter to the black tree's will.

She moved through the town like a shadow, unseen, unheard, until she reached the next farmhouse's door. The occupants had barricaded themselves inside, windows boarded, a weak attempt to keep out the darkness. But the black tree's hunger knew no bounds, and neither did her power now.

With a soft, unnatural creak, the door opened at her touch, revealing her siblings huddled together, pale and trembling, their faces lined with fear as they recognized her. They barely recognized her—their sister had become a stranger, something other, a creature born of the wild and claimed by the darkness.

One of her brothers whispered her name, as if calling it would remind her of who she once was. But she felt nothing—no tug of recognition, no kinship. She was bound to the black tree now, and her purpose was clear.

"You don't belong here anymore," her eldest sibling said, voice shaking, as if he could make her leave with just words. She tilted her head, a predatory glint in her eyes, and took a slow, deliberate step forward.

"You belong to the forest," she said, her voice low and cold, echoing the whisper of the tree. "Just as I do."

They scrambled to the back of the room, clinging to each other, their fear palpable, feeding the darkness within her. She felt herself revel in it, felt her teeth sharpen as her lips pulled back in a twisted smile. There was a cruel pleasure in their terror, a satisfaction that ran deeper than human understanding.

One by one, she extended her hand to each of them, feeling the shadow pass from her fingers to them. They shivered, eyes widening as the black tree's roots took hold, weaving through their minds, binding them as it had bound her.

A single tear fell down the cheek of her younger sister as she mouthed, "Please..."

But there was no mercy left in her heart. She belonged to the black tree, and so would they. The legend had claimed her, and now it demanded they follow, all souls united under the same shadow.

The black tree's hunger would not be sated until every last one had returned to its roots. And as she stood there, watching the light fade from her siblings' eyes, she knew that the town—their lives—would soon follow, swallowed whole by the darkness she had unleashed.

The farmhouse grew colder, as if every trace of warmth had been sucked out, replaced by a chill that seemed to emanate from her very presence. Her siblings' breaths came in shallow gasps, their eyes dulling, limbs shaking as they felt the shadows wrap around them like a shroud. Her own form grew darker, the shadow deepening in her eyes as she let the black tree's will pour through her, the force of it pressing against her siblings' minds and draining their resistance.

The walls of the farmhouse trembled, groaning under the weight of an unseen force. Blackened roots crept in through the cracks, twisting and coiling, reaching like skeletal hands for her siblings. The roots latched onto their ankles, pulling them down, grounding them to the spot as though binding them to the forest's ancient curse.

A low hum filled the room, an echo of something far older than the tree, a vibration that carried the weight of centuries. Her siblings stared in horror as the roots wound around them, like veins of the earth itself come to reclaim them. They struggled, but every movement was met with resistance, the roots tightening, pressing against their skin with unrelenting force.

She took a step back, watching with an expression that held only cold, detached fascination. The darkness in her eyes deepened, her face void of any recognition, any empathy. In that moment, she was no longer the sister they had known but the embodiment of the forest's will, the keeper of the black tree's insatiable hunger.

As the roots dragged them down, her siblings cried out, their voices hoarse, their pleas growing softer, drowned out by the pulse of the tree. The shadows seemed to thicken, absorbing their cries as though the very air had turned solid and impenetrable, swallowing all sound.

Through it all, the tree's voice echoed in her mind, soothing and cold, filling her with a sense of purpose that was both exhilarating and terrifying. They were meant to return, it whispered. They were always meant to be mine.

When the last of her siblings fell silent, their forms cradled by the roots, she felt a twisted satisfaction settle within her. She could feel their essence flowing back into the forest, each life becoming part of the black tree's roots, strengthening it, feeding its unyielding hunger.

A ripple spread through the forest, a dark energy pulsing outward, reaching the very edges of the town. Animals fell silent, their instincts warning them to flee, while the townspeople stirred, an unshakable dread taking hold. Something fundamental had shifted, a darkness seeping into the earth itself, binding it to her, to the tree, to the ancient promise she had now fulfilled.

She stepped back into the woods, her transformation complete, the shadows dancing around her as though recognizing her as their queen, their keeper. She was no longer bound by human needs, no longer tethered by the ties of family or memory. She was a creature of the wild, a vessel of darkness, the 13th child claimed by the woods.

And as she walked deeper into the shadows, she felt the black tree's roots weaving through her very soul, tying her forever to its dark heart, an unbreakable bond that would persist long after the town was nothing but ruins, swallowed by the creeping forest that would spread, inch by inch, claiming all that dared come close.

Chapter 23: The Devil's Due

The townspeople gathered in a dimly lit basement beneath the oldest church, its stone walls bearing the weight of generations' fears and whispered legends. Oil lanterns cast flickering shadows, illuminating the faces of the men and women huddled close, their eyes darting nervously as if the darkness itself were watching.

At the center of the room, the town's oldest resident, an ancient woman named Hester with eyes clouded by time, began to speak in a voice as frail as the autumn leaves outside. "It is as the old tales have warned us. The forest has claimed the 13th child, born in darkness and bound to it. And once the forest takes them…" Her voice wavered, her face twisting in fear. "It molds them into something else. A daemon. A devil."

The villagers exchanged glances, fear visible in every line etched on their faces. The legend of the 13th child was one they had all grown up hearing, a dark tale whispered to children to keep them from venturing too far into the forest. But now, that tale had come to life, a nightmarish prophecy fulfilled in the form of the girl who had become a creature of shadows.

"She was one of our own," muttered one of the men, shaking his head as if refusing to believe the transformation. "I remember her playing by the river, laughing, she was just a child…"

"But the woods don't care," Hester interrupted sharply, her voice harder now, betraying the fear she held back. "The 13th child is not like any other. In every generation, if the line holds, a 13th child born within these lands is claimed by the forest. It shapes them, twists them, until they're no longer bound by human laws."

Hester's wrinkled hands trembled as she continued. "The forest doesn't simply claim them; it merges them with something darker. They become its spirit, its eyes, its claws in the world of the living. The 13th child becomes the daemon of the woods—a protector and a curse."

One of the younger villagers leaned forward, his voice barely a whisper. "But there must be a way to stop it. Can't we… take back what the woods have taken? Bring her out?"

Hester shook her head solemnly. "No one has ever returned from the forest once claimed. There's no power strong enough to sever the bond between the 13th child and the woods. They become part of the forest's very roots, their blood woven into its dark soul."

A silence settled over the room, as thick and suffocating as the mist outside. Each villager grappled with the legend that had haunted their town for centuries. In every generation, the black tree's hunger awakened, waiting, watching, for the 13th child—a vessel it could fill with its ancient malice.

Another villager, his voice trembling, spoke up. "But if the daemon has come into our town... if she's already taken others..." His eyes darted to the door, as if the girl might emerge from the shadows at any moment. "What can we do? How can we protect ourselves?"

Hester's gaze was distant, her mind turning over memories long buried. "There are rites, old as the forest itself. Rituals meant to ward off the 13th child's influence. But these things require a sacrifice—a blood offering that binds the forest's curse."

The villagers recoiled, fear gripping them anew. Blood sacrifices were whispered about, stories from generations past when the forest's wrath had stirred before. They knew that the ancient forest did not release its claims easily, and to appease it required a payment that none were eager to make.

A young woman, voice shaking with desperation, asked, "Then... then what hope do we have? Are we to just wait, trapped, until she comes for us all?"

Hester's mouth twisted in sorrow. "If we do nothing, she will come. The daemon has tasted the lives it was promised. If we don't appease it, she won't stop. The forest will spread, swallowing all in its path, and none of us will be spared."

The tension in the room grew thick as the weight of the legend settled over them, the reality of their plight sinking in. The daemon was not some distant horror; it was a child born among them, twisted into something unholy by the very land they lived on. And now, bound by ancient rites and curses, they faced the impossible choice.

The oldest among them finally spoke, breaking the silence. "We must choose," he said grimly, his voice barely above a whisper. "Either we give the forest what it craves, or we all fall prey to it."

They all knew what he meant—the curse required blood to bind it, a life to seal it back into the woods. But who among them would bear that terrible weight? And who would decide who would give their life to halt the 13th child's dark reign?

Each face was a mask of terror as they looked between one another, knowing that this would be a night none of them would escape unscathed. And as they deliberated in hushed voices, the darkness outside seemed to press closer, watching, waiting for the blood it had been promised.

The village was cast in a mournful silence as word spread of the gathering. Families locked their doors, candles flickered in windows, and a stillness descended, broken only by the creak of trees swaying outside, as if even they held their breath. Shadows crept over the town, watching as the villagers moved like specters through the night, each drawn by a grim sense of duty, a silent understanding that their survival now depended on sacrifice.

Inside the old church basement, the villagers' fear had transformed into a shared determination, an unspoken pact bound by the threat that lurked within the woods. Hester's voice cut through the silence, weathered but steady, as she relayed what little they knew about the old rites, passed down through generations like secrets best kept hidden.

"There must be a chosen one," she murmured, her gaze sweeping the faces of those gathered. "The sacrifice must be willing, for only a willing heart can seal the forest's hunger. A ritual of binding, an exchange to satisfy the forest's curse."

Murmurs of disbelief and quiet sobs filled the room as her words settled over them like a shroud. Willing. The word echoed in their minds. Who among them would be willing to face the terror in those dark woods?

Eyes turned to the older men and women, those who had lived long and believed their lives nearing their end, but each face remained blank, distant. Hester's voice cut through the silence again. "A life given freely will hold the curse... for a time. But only blood of the land can silence it for good."

The cryptic words sank in slowly, and realization dawned on the villagers as they looked toward one another in horror. Only one of their own, bound by blood to the land, could offer themselves fully to the woods. It wasn't just a life; it had to be someone connected to the land, someone whose roots tied them to the town's history.

And that left only a few names on everyone's mind. The family that had lived closest to the woods, the family with the daughter—the one they had all whispered about, the one the forest had already claimed.

The choice weighed heavily, but the fear of what might come if they did nothing was stronger.

"We must go to them," Hester said finally, her voice weary, but resolved. "We must ask."

A shudder ran through the room as they rose, torches in hand, their footsteps heavy as they prepared to approach Evelyn and her father, and present them with an unspeakable choice.

As the villagers moved toward the family's cabin, their torches casting eerie shadows on the forest floor, a quiet dread settled over them. The trees loomed taller, their branches twisting above like skeletal fingers reaching toward the sky. The silence of the forest was thick, unnatural, as though every creature had stilled, sensing the disturbance that pulsed through the air.

The cabin sat on the edge of the village, dark and weathered, bearing the weight of the woods that loomed close around it. It was clear they'd long since withdrawn from the townsfolk, estranged and distant, choosing the solitude of the woods over the company of their neighbors. Yet, tonight, there was no escape from what the village demanded.

Hester stepped forward, knocking on the cabin door with a hand that trembled. The door creaked open, and Evelyn stood in the entryway, her face drawn and weary, a shadow of resignation in her eyes. She knew why they had come. She had heard the whispers in town, the way eyes followed her when she went to market. And deep down, she knew it would come to this—the legacy of the 13th child, a prophecy she had tried to ignore but could no longer escape.

The villagers stepped back, their eyes averted, ashamed, yet unwilling to relent. Hester cleared her throat, her voice brittle in the cold night air. "We... we know what the woods have done. We know what your sister has become," she whispered, choosing her words carefully. "The curse has awoken, and the forest's hunger will not be satisfied until..." Her voice trailed off, but everyone knew what she meant.

Evelyn's face twisted with grief, but she remained silent, her gaze fixed on the woods beyond. Her eyes held a strange sadness, as though she understood the forest's dark pull all too well, perhaps even sympathized with it. She nodded slowly, resigned, and closed the door behind her. The villagers waited in tense silence as she disappeared inside, steeling themselves for the impossible choice they had demanded her to make.

Minutes later, the door creaked open once more, and she re-emerged, leading her father by the hand. He was a frail thing, worn and broken. He refused to leave the cabin after his child, his youngest daughter, stayed in the pines. He refused to leave after his wife grew ill and died from a broken heart. He refused to leave even when all but one of his children abandoned all hope and moved into the village.

Evelyn spoke softly, her voice breaking as she met Hester's gaze. "If we, our family are truly bound to the forest, then let it be my sisters choice. Let her decide. We will both go willingly."

Evelyn glanced at her father, his wild eyes narrowing, and for a brief moment, there was a flicker of something—confusion, perhaps, or even defiance. He understood the call of the forest, felt its pull deep within his veins, but now he sensed the cost, the sacrifice the village demanded. Evelyn looked out into the woods, where shadows pooled and shifted, beckoning her and her father forward, promising secrets only she could understand.

Without a word, she stepped down and away from the cabin door taking her fathers hand and took a hesitant step toward the trees, then another. The villagers watched, transfixed, as she and her father moved with a strange, almost reverent grace, the darkness folding around them like a shroud. Her fathers face twisted with grief, his hand clasped tightly to Evelyn's as they disappeared into the night.

The villagers knew this was the moment of reckoning, the answer to the curse that haunted them all. With each step they took, they felt the weight of the forest's hunger begin to shift, its restless power acknowledging their choice, accepting them as its own.

But as they vanished into the shadows, a terrible realization settled over the villagers. The forest would always demand more, its hunger unending. They had given it what it asked for—this time—but they all understood that this sacrifice would only buy them a brief reprieve.

Chapter 24: The Binding

Evelyn knew that the burden of the curse had not been lifted, only temporarily placated. She felt its weight pressing into her, a constant, gnawing presence in the back of her mind. In her dreams, the trees whispered, and the shadow that haunted the woods took form—something ancient and ravenous, a creature that called itself by no name, for there was none dark enough to describe it.

Each night, the presence grew stronger, the connection deeper, until Evelyn understood what the forest demanded. The dark force would not be appeased until it had a soul bound willingly, a life tied to the earth forever. She knew that her father could not carry this burden; his mind, already slipping, would one day be fully claimed by the shadows of grief.

And so, she made her choice.

In a small hallow, near the edge of the woods she led her father and set him down on a moss covered log. Then Evelyn set out alone into the darkness, moving silently through the pines as it pressed in on her. She carried only a small lantern, its faint glow casting long shadows across her face, illuminating the fierce resolve in her eyes. The woods rose up around her, alive with the sounds of the night, as if sensing her arrival and preparing for the offering she was about to make.

At the heart of the forest stood the black tree—the one her sister had summoned from the depths of the earth, twisted and looming, its branches stretching like skeletal fingers toward the sky. A cold wind swept through the clearing, carrying with it the scent of decay and something ancient, older than the soil it stood upon.

Evelyn approached, her breaths shallow, feeling the cold seeping into her bones as she stood before the tree. A shiver ran through her as the ground beneath her feet began to pulse, a heartbeat in sync with the forest itself. She closed her eyes, summoning the courage she needed, and spoke aloud, her voice trembling but determined.

"I give myself to you," she whispered. "Take me instead of my father. I offer my life, my soul, to satisfy the hunger that stirs within these woods."

The forest responded immediately. The air thickened, becoming almost oppressive, and a deep, guttural rumble rose from beneath the earth, as if the forest itself had heard her and was considering her sacrifice. The black tree seemed to sway, its branches creaking as if acknowledging her presence, and the darkness deepened, swirling around her like a living thing.

Suddenly, the ground beneath her feet split open, revealing a chasm that led down into an abyss of roots and shadows. She hesitated, feeling the pull of the earth, the invitation to descend into the heart of the forest itself, where the dark force awaited her.

With one last glance at the night sky, she stepped forward, allowing herself to be swallowed by the earth. The darkness closed around her, cold and unforgiving, as she descended into the depths, her heartbeat slowing, merging with the rhythm of the forest.

At the end of her descent, she found herself in a cavern lit by the sickly glow of bioluminescent fungi. Shadows danced along the walls, and in the center of the chamber loomed a figure—a Daemon, a creature of darkness made flesh. It had no clear form, shifting and twisting with each breath, its eyes burning with an otherworldly light that pierced through her.

Evelyn stood before it, her resolve unwavering, and knelt in the damp earth, bowing her head in submission. "I am yours," she murmured, feeling the weight of her words settle over her. "Take my life as payment, but release the village from your grip."

The Daemon's laughter echoed through the cavern, a sound both chilling and seductive, filling her with a sense of dread that twisted deep within her soul. It moved closer, its shifting form towering over her, and extended a shadowed hand to touch her forehead.

"You offer yourself willingly," it whispered, its voice like the rustling of dead leaves. "But know this: once given, your soul will be bound here, tethered to the forest for eternity. You will become part of me, part of the hunger that drives these woods. Do you understand?"

The sister nodded, swallowing her fear. "I understand. I am ready."

With a final, chilling smile, the Daemon pressed its hand against her chest, and she felt a searing pain as her soul was torn from her body, merging with the darkness that surrounded her. Her consciousness flickered, fading, as she became one with the forest, her thoughts dissolving into shadows, her essence bound to the ancient hunger that would forever haunt the woods.

The 13th child had felt the call of the black tree as a deep, pulsing throb in her veins. She moved silently through the forest, her bare feet navigating the roots and thorns that others would stumble upon, her body agile and primal. Her mind, now fully entwined with the forest's dark spirit, was no longer bound by the confines of humanity. She was part animal, part force of nature, and wholly bound to the ancient power that had claimed her from birth.

When she arrived at the black tree, the air was thick with an unnatural stillness. She sensed her sister's presence—felt it in a way that sent a strange thrill through her. It had been a long time since she had felt the pull of her family, and yet here it was, tied to this place of shadows and silence, drawing her in like a scent on the wind. Her lips curled in a crooked smile, feral and triumphant, as she saw her sister standing at the base of the twisted tree, her hands clenched tightly, her face pale in the sickly glow that radiated from the roots.

The feral girl slipped into the shadows, watching with hungry curiosity as her sister knelt before the black tree, the air around her growing colder, heavier. She could feel the anticipation, the offering that her sister was making. And instead of anger or sorrow, she felt a dark satisfaction. Her sister had come to join her here, to be part of the woods just as she was. They would be bound together at last, woven into the same shadows, bound by blood and earth.

As the ritual began, she watched with a strange delight as the Daemon—the shadowy force she had come to recognize as a part of herself—descended upon her sister. Its form shifted, murky and undefined, tendrils of darkness creeping around her sister's wrists and ankles, binding her to the tree. Her sister's face twisted in pain, her body writhing as the Daemon's shadows seeped into her, consuming her spirit.

The feral girl's smile widened. There was a twisted satisfaction in seeing her sister writhe, seeing her become part of the forest in a way that was painful, inevitable. She understood now, as she watched her sister's struggle, that the darkness of the woods demanded sacrifice. Her sister's pain, her screams, were offerings to the tree, tributes to the Daemon that ruled the shadows.

But there was something more—a flicker of connection that the feral girl hadn't expected. As her sister's life was drained, her own bond with the forest grew stronger. She felt her mind meld further with the Daemon's, her own heartbeat syncing with the ancient rhythm of the woods, her vision blurring as she merged with the darkness. She could taste the sorrow, the anger, and the anguish that filled her sister's spirit, and it felt like a feast.

As the final moments came, her sister's gaze caught her own, a mix of agony and recognition in her eyes. It was as though her sister had finally seen her for what she was:

the wild child, the 13th one, the cursed daughter of the woods. And in that last moment, she saw something else—a flicker of betrayal, a flash of despair. It lingered in the air between them, a silent accusation, before her sister's eyes went blank, her spirit forever bound to the black tree.

The feral girl tilted her head, watching as the last remnants of her sister's humanity faded into the shadows, swallowed whole by the forest's insatiable hunger. She felt no regret, no sorrow. This was the way of the woods, the way of the darkness that coursed through her veins. And now, with her sister's spirit bound to the black tree, her own power pulsed stronger than ever, her form shifting subtly, becoming something darker, something more monstrous.

For the first time, she felt complete, a creature of the woods in every way. She turned from the black tree, her mind a twisted fusion of beast and shadow, and disappeared into the night, leaving only silence in her wake.

Chapter 25: The Whispering Grove

The forest had changed. In the wake of the ritual, a restless energy pulsed through the woods, as though the shadows themselves had been awakened and were now watching, waiting. The trees whispered secrets with each breeze, their voices low and sinister, filling the air with an unnatural tension that crept along the forest floor. Those who dared to venture close to the treeline felt it—a chill that seeped into their bones, a sense of something darker than night itself lying just beyond their sight.

The feral girl moved through the trees, her senses sharpened, her awareness attuned to every shift in the shadows. She felt the forest's new life as if it were her own, the beating pulse of the black tree resonating with each step. Her transformation had taken her beyond human limitations; she was no longer merely a girl, nor was she simply a beast. She was something more—a creature born of earth and spirit, of darkness and sacrifice. She was bound to the woods, and they to her.

But as powerful as she felt, there was an itch in the back of her mind, a fragment of humanity lingering, like a thorn buried deep within her. The image of her sister's face, twisted with pain and betrayal, flashed in her memory. It was as if her sister's spirit still clung to her, a reminder of what she had given up, a faint whisper of guilt she couldn't quite shake. She growled, trying to banish the thought, but it lingered like an echo in the dark, a ghost of her own making.

She wandered deeper into the forest, seeking the silence, the solitude that would drown out these intrusions. But the deeper she went, the louder the whispers grew, as if the woods themselves were speaking to her, calling her toward something unknown. The ground was littered with twisted roots and decaying leaves, and the air smelled of damp earth and rot, heavy and suffocating.

Then, as if in response to her silent question, the forest shifted. Shadows gathered, pooling at the base of the towering black tree. The darkness thickened, forming a shape—a figure that seemed to rise from the earth itself, its body made of writhing shadows and cold, empty light. The figure's face was obscured, but its eyes were unmistakable: dark, unblinking, and filled with an ancient, malevolent knowledge.

The girl stood frozen, a sense of awe and terror washing over her. She knew this presence, felt it in the marrow of her bones. It was the Daemon, the spirit of the forest that had claimed her, bound her, and twisted her soul. She felt her own darkness swell in response, a sinister thrill as their energies intertwined, a rush of power and fear that surged through her veins.

The Daemon's voice was a low hiss, a murmur of death and decay that echoed in her mind. "You are mine," it whispered, a promise and a threat all at once. "You have always been mine, from the moment you drew your first breath beneath these trees. The blood that runs in your veins is my own."

The feral girl felt a shiver run down her spine, a thrill of understanding. She had always known, on some level, that she was bound to this place, but now she saw it in full. She was the 13th child, a child of prophecy and blood, marked by the forest's ancient curse. Her life was no longer her own; she was an extension of the forest's will, a creature of shadow and sacrifice. And as much as she had resisted it, she now felt herself surrendering, her mind bending to the Daemon's dark intentions.

"What would you have me do?" she whispered, her voice barely a breath, yet filled with dark resolve.

The Daemon's gaze deepened, shadows swirling around them both as it leaned close, its voice a rasp that clawed at her mind. "The forest is hungry, my child. Feed it. Give it the blood it craves, the lives it demands. Only then will the hunger be sated. Only then will you truly belong."

The girl's smile was cold, devoid of any lingering trace of humanity. She understood now. The forest had always demanded sacrifices, lives for the life it gave her, blood for the power it bestowed. Her family had given her this gift, and she would honor it—she would become the creature the Daemon wanted her to be, a reaper in the shadows, a hunter in the night.

She nodded, feeling the weight of her new purpose settle within her like a second heartbeat. And as she turned and melted into the darkness, the whispers of the forest grew louder, filling the night with the sound of promises and curses, of secrets kept and horrors yet to come. The trees closed around her, their shadows reaching out, welcoming her as one of their own.

The hunt had begun. And the woods, hungry and waiting, echoed her every step.

As the feral girl prowled through the underbrush, her senses pricked at the faint sound of movement nearby. She stilled, inhaling deeply, drawing in the scent of her surroundings—the damp moss, the rich, loamy earth, and something else: the familiar, faint scent of human sweat, tinged with desperation. Her pulse quickened, her instincts stirring with the thrill of the hunt. She knew this scent. It was him.

Her father.

She crept forward, silent as the shadows, her eyes scanning the dense woods. And there he was, stumbling through the twisted trees, his face drawn and tired, his eyes searching desperately, scanning the darkened forest with the haunted look of a man possessed. He was calling out, his voice barely more than a rasp as he repeated her name and her sister's, his words tumbling out in fragments, pleading and panicked.

"Please... if you can hear me... come back. Just come home. We'll... we'll make it right... I'll make it right..."

His words washed over her like the breeze through the trees, meaningless and distant, something she could no longer connect to or understand. She watched him, curiosity mingling with a sense of detachment, as if she were observing an animal caught in a trap. Once, she might have felt a pang of something at his voice—a remnant of a bond that had long since unraveled. But now, standing in the shadows with the forest alive and breathing around her, those emotions were nothing more than hollow echoes.

Yet as she watched him stumble, the Daemon's words pulsed in her mind, urging her onward. The forest was hungry, and she was its instrument, bound to serve its insatiable needs. Her father's fear, his guilt, they would only feed the woods' appetite. A chill ran through her, a sense of dark satisfaction settling over her, and she felt herself smile, a twisted, feral grin that bared her teeth.

She moved closer, her body silent and lithe, hidden beneath the cloak of shadows. She could see him more clearly now—the lines etched into his face, the dark hollows under his eyes. There was a rawness to him, a vulnerability she had never seen before, as if the forest itself had worn him down, stripped him of his resolve and left him broken, grasping at the impossible hope that he might still save his lost children.

For a brief, fleeting moment, something flickered in her mind—a memory of his voice, strong and steady, guiding her through the woods when she was young, teaching her to respect the land, to move silently, to listen. But as quickly as it came, the memory faded, replaced by the creeping darkness, by the whispers that promised power and belonging. She was no longer that child; she had become something else entirely.

She circled him, staying just beyond the edges of his vision, watching as his despair deepened. She could sense his fear now, could see the tremor in his hands, the way his gaze darted through the shadows as though he felt her presence but couldn't quite place it. The forest amplified his fear, warping sounds and shapes around him, feeding off his dread. She felt her own excitement build, a savage thrill that urged her forward, closer, ready to see him fall, to make him understand what she had become.

Finally, she stepped into his line of sight, her figure barely more than a wraith among the trees. His eyes locked onto her, and for a moment, disbelief crossed his face. He took a step forward, his voice choked and trembling.

"My girl... you... you're alive," he whispered, a spark of hope flickering in his gaze.

But there was nothing left in her to answer that hope. She simply stared, her expression blank, her eyes dark and unreadable, her face marked by subtle changes—her skin pale as the moonlight filtering through the trees, her eyes sharper, almost feral, and her posture tense, coiled like an animal ready to strike. She was no longer the daughter he had once known; she was something ancient, something born of the forest's shadow.

As he took another hesitant step, reaching a hand out, the forest itself seemed to recoil, the shadows deepening, gathering around her like a shroud. The air grew thick, charged with an energy that prickled along her skin, and a voice echoed in her mind—a voice as dark as the depths of the woods, urging her forward, commanding her to fulfill her purpose.

Her father stopped, his hand falling to his side as the realization dawned on him. The hope drained from his face, replaced by horror and resignation. He seemed to sag under the weight of it, his shoulders slumping as he whispered, more to himself than to her, "What have you become?"

She tilted her head, considering his question, but no answer came. Instead, she stepped back into the shadows, leaving him standing alone in the clearing, swallowed by his own despair. She turned and vanished into the trees, letting the darkness consume her, the whispers of the forest guiding her as she left her father to face his own demons amid the haunted woods.

The forest would take him, just as it had taken her. And with each step, she felt herself slipping further, the last vestiges of her old life disappearing, replaced by the savage promise of the shadows.

Chapter 26: Final Chapter: The Price of Blood

The forest was silent, a dreadful stillness hanging in the air as though even the trees held their breath. The dark branches loomed like the skeletal fingers of ancient hands, reaching, grasping, waiting for the final act to unfold. The black tree in the center of the forest, pulsing with an otherworldly energy, had absorbed the offerings of her siblings—those who had fled but could not escape its call, its hunger. Her sister had come willingly, a lamb to the slaughter, and now only her father remained.

The feral girl, the 13th child of the woods, stood near the twisted trunk, her body a vessel for the forest's relentless will. She felt no sadness, no pangs of regret. Her father was a shadow of what he had once been, reduced to a wandering soul who had spent his last hope on something that no longer existed. He was merely the final piece, the last thread to sever, to fulfill her purpose and complete the prophecy.

As she waited, she could feel the Daemon's presence coiling around her, a weight that pressed down on her like a living shadow. The being had been her guide, her companion in the dark transformation, whispering secrets of the woods, of blood, of sacrifice. Its voice echoed now in her mind, low and serpentine, a murmur of satisfaction.

"He comes, child. He comes to you, knowing nothing of what awaits."

She lifted her gaze to the path, and, as if on command, her father emerged, stumbling into the clearing. His eyes, wide with terror and sorrow, locked onto her. He looked like he hadn't slept in days; his skin was pale and drawn, his clothes were tattered, and his gaze held a fractured look, like a man who had seen too many horrors but couldn't turn away. His breaths were shallow, his body trembling as he realized where he had wandered.

"You... my daughter..." he choked, as though the very words were foreign to him now. He looked at her, at the girl who had once been his child and was now something twisted and unrecognizable.

"Yes," she said softly, her voice as hollow and cold as the night. "I am your daughter. But I am also more."

He staggered, the weight of the forest pressing in around him. The dark trees leaned closer, like voyeurs to his suffering, their shadows creeping toward him with eager hunger. The air grew colder, sharper, thick with the promise of violence.

Her father dropped to his knees, as if something in the weight of her gaze had broken him. "Please," he begged, his voice cracking. "Whatever this is... let it end. Let this curse die with me."

But the Daemon's voice slithered into her mind once more, rich with its insatiable desire. "No mercy. You are the 13th child, the darkness reborn. Fulfill your purpose."

She took a step forward, her eyes empty as she watched her father's face collapse into despair. She could feel the pull of the black tree behind her, the yawning abyss of its ancient hunger, the relentless call that echoed through her very blood. The prophecy demanded his life, his essence, to solidify the bond that tied her to this place forever.

As she advanced, her father's hands shot out, grasping for something, anything to hold onto. He looked at her with a heartbreaking mixture of love and horror, seeing not the feral creature she had become but the ghost of the daughter he had once known.

"No... please..." he whispered.

But she was beyond mercy, beyond the reach of his love or his pleas. The Daemon surged forward through her, wrapping her in its shadow, fueling her transformation. Her teeth sharpened, her nails lengthened, and her eyes glinted with an animalistic hunger. The darkness wrapped around her, fusing her fully with the malevolent force that had always waited, lurking beneath the forest's roots.

With one swift motion, she reached out and grasped his arm, pulling him to her. Her strength was inhuman, her grip unbreakable. He gasped, his voice no more than a broken whisper as he struggled against her.

"This is the price," she intoned, her voice carrying the weight of countless souls that had been lost to the woods, the echo of the generations that had come before her. "The forest demands its due."

The black tree groaned as though alive, its twisted branches writhing in anticipation. The shadows seemed to throb with a life of their own, and the Daemon's laughter rumbled through the clearing, triumphant and terrible.

With a final, anguished scream, her father was pulled from her grasp, as though the very forest itself had reached out to claim him. The shadows enveloped him, consuming him, his cries fading into the endless dark until there was nothing left but silence.

The feral girl, now fully transformed, stood alone before the black tree, feeling the weight of her sacrifice settle within her. She had fulfilled the prophecy; she was the 13th child, the darkness given flesh, and her bond to the forest was eternal. The Daemon's whispers faded, replaced by an overwhelming quiet that seeped into her bones, anchoring her to this place, this cursed land that would forever be her home.

As dawn broke and a pale light filtered through the trees, she remained rooted there, a part of the forest, a shadow among shadows. And as the years passed, legends would grow of a dark figure haunting the Pine Barrens, a feral creature with eyes that glowed like embers, the 13th child who had given herself over to the woods, forever lost but forever watching, the eternal guardian of the forest's malevolent heart.

Epilogue

In the shadows of New Jersey's Pine Barrens, there is a legend as deep-rooted as the forest itself: the story of the Jersey Devil, a creature of myth, mystery, and terror. According to folklore, the Jersey Devil was the 13th child of Mother Leeds, a woman who, when faced with the birth of her thirteenth child, cursed the child in a moment of desperation. Her words bound the child to the darkest corners of the Barrens, transforming it into a beast—part human, part animal, and fully bound to the woods.

This child, they say, was born with leathery wings, cloven hooves, and a piercing scream that could freeze a man's heart. Since its birth, stories tell of its haunting presence stalking the forests, an eerie echo in the night, a shadow between the trees. For centuries, locals have shared tales of strange sightings and unexplainable sounds in the Barrens, all attributed to this dark creature—the devil of the forest.

In this story, the 13th child is an echo of that original legend, a modern reinterpretation of a dark birthright. But rather than the physical transformation of the Leeds child into the Jersey Devil, our 13th child is transformed by the forest itself, slowly shaped by the whispers and ancient forces of the woods. This tale draws upon the primal fears of isolation and the unknown, where the sinister beauty of nature merges with the twisted bonds of family and legacy.

As she grew and took on the identity foretold for her, the 13th child embodied the same eerie, sinister connection to the Pine Barrens as the Jersey Devil. Like the original creature of legend, she becomes a part of the forest's shadow, feared and shunned by those who know the stories. Her journey from feral innocence to becoming the spirit of the Barrens is a parallel to the original curse—a reminder of how fear and myth can transform a life into something darker, and how the woods remember every secret, every curse, and every life given to it.

Perhaps she is a descendant of the Jersey Devil, perhaps just a spirit reborn, but in the end, she fulfills the prophecy in her own way. The Barrens, once more, have claimed their 13th child.

Dear Reader,

Thank you for joining me on this journey through the dark heart of the Pine Barrens. Growing up in southern New Jersey, I was surrounded by tales of the Jersey Devil and the mysteries of these woods. As a child, I was drawn to the wild beauty of the Pine Barrens, wandering the trails and listening to the whispers of the pines, never quite knowing if they were real or imagined.

There were days when the woods seemed friendly, welcoming even, as sunlight slipped through the branches and the familiar calls of wildlife echoed around me. But there were other days—still, heavy days—when I felt as if something unseen was watching, a silent presence that followed me in the shadows. I can recall moments of chilling stillness, where even the air felt tense, thick with something ancient, as if I'd stumbled upon a hidden truth that wasn't meant for me.

On one such afternoon, I lost my way in an unfamiliar part of the forest. The further I walked, the quieter it became, the usual sounds of the woods replaced by an eerie silence. That was the first time I felt it—a pull, as if something deeper in the woods was calling to me. I ran back to the familiar paths, but the memory of that strange moment stayed with me, as if the forest had whispered a secret it would only half reveal.

These experiences planted the seeds for this story and gave life to my own tale of the 13th child. As I wrote, I found myself reflecting on the timelessness of those legends and the uneasy relationship between humanity and nature. To this day, I can't say whether the woods are truly haunted by something sinister or if it's simply the power of storytelling that keeps these legends alive.

Whether you believe in curses, in dark forests filled with mysteries, or in the uncanny presence of the Jersey Devil, I hope this book has given you a sense of the Pine Barrens' magic and dread. The woods have a way of holding onto secrets, and I believe that each of us, in some way, carries a piece of that mystery with us.

Thank you for stepping into the Pine Barrens with me. The shadows will remember.

With gratitude and a shared thirst for the thrill,

Monica Lynne Chase

Made in the USA
Middletown, DE
08 November 2024

64151836R00057